THIS IS NOT AN ORDINARY COMIC!

In *Meanwhile*, YOU make the choices that determine how the story unfolds. Instead of one story, *Meanwhile* splits off into thousands of different adventures. Most will end in DOOM and DISASTER. Only one path will lead you to happiness and success.

To read *Meanwhile*, remember that each panel is connected to the next by a thin tube. The tubes may travel right to left, left to right, top to bottom, or bottom to top—so be sure to keep your eye on where the tube is taking you.

Sometimes a tube splits into two paths. When this happens, YOU, the reader, get to choose which path to follow.

Other times a tube leads off the page and onto a tab on a different page. When that happens, simply turn to the tabbed page without flipping it over and follow the tube onto that new page.

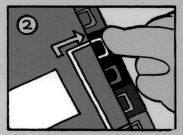

Meanwhile also contains codes that allow you access to top-secret pages. If you come across a page that asks for such a code, you may feel tempted to look through the book out of order or guess until you find the correct one. But cheaters only cheat themselves. Instead, try backtracking or starting a new adventure, and see if you can find a way to discover the code on your own.

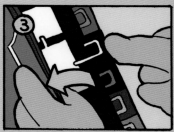

Finally, remember that *Meanwhile* is different from any other book you've read before. But it's also more fun. With perseverance and curiosity, you too can unlock the book's secrets and find your way home. Good luck, and choose wisely!

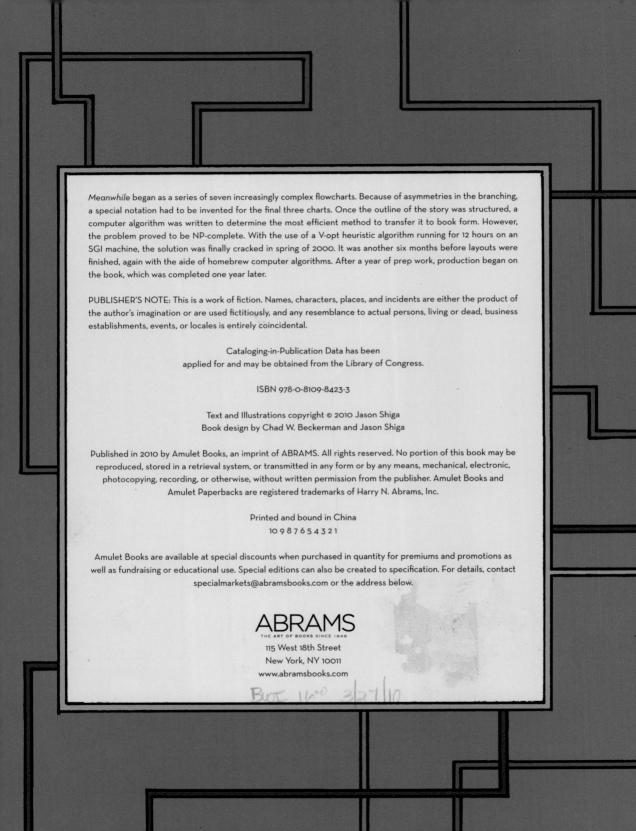

Meanwhile began as a series of seven increasingly complex flowcharts. Because of asymmetries in the branching, a special notation had to be invented for the final three charts. Once the outline of the story was structured, a computer algorithm was written to determine the most efficient method to transfer it to book form. However, the problem proved to be NP-complete. With the use of a V-opt heuristic algorithm running for 12 hours on an SGI machine, the solution was finally cracked in spring of 2000. It was another six months before layouts were finished, again with the aide of homebrew computer algorithms. After a year of prep work, production began on the book, which was completed one year later.

Cataloging-in-Publication Data has been
applied for and may be obtained from the Library of Congress.

ISBN 978-0-8109-8423-3

Printed and bound in China
10 9 8 7 6 5 4 3 2 1

Amulet Books are available at special discounts when purchased in quantity for premiums and promotions as well as fundraising or educational use. Special editions can also be created to specification. For details, contact specialmarkets@abramsbooks.com or the address below.

ABRAMS
THE ART OF BOOKS SINCE 1949
115 West 18th Street
New York, NY 10011
www.abramsbooks.com

Buot 16⁰⁰ 3/27/10

For my Mom and Dad

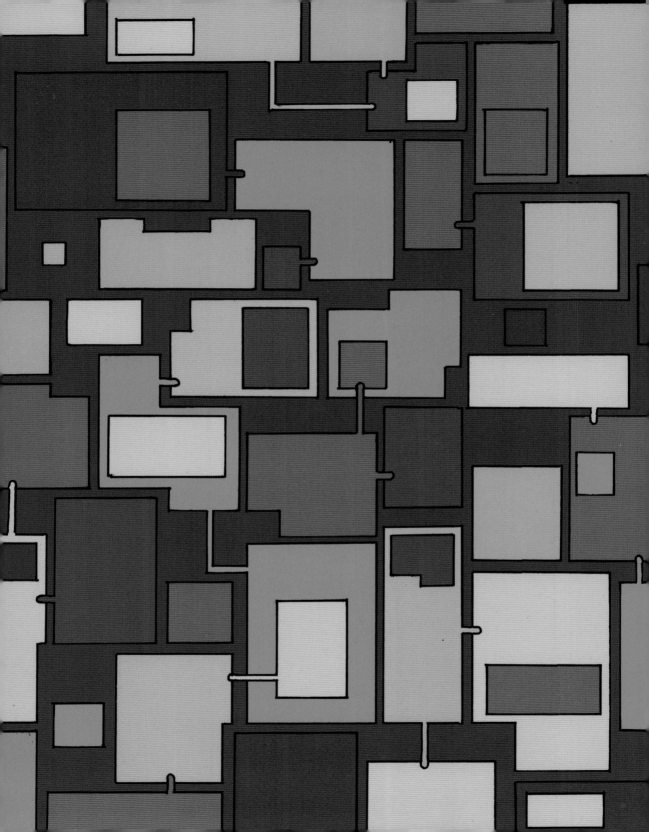

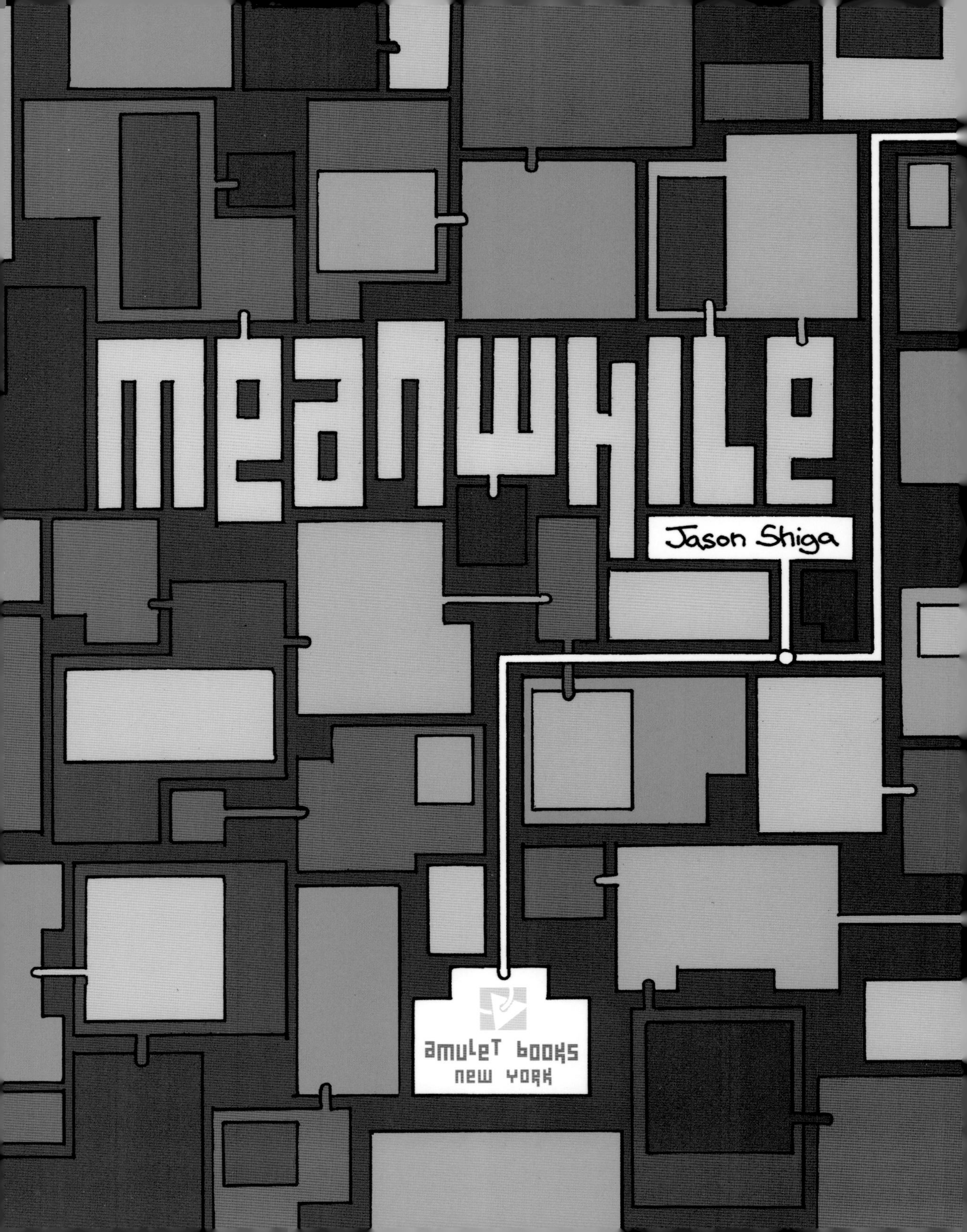

MEANWHILE
Jason Shiga
amulet books
NEW YORK

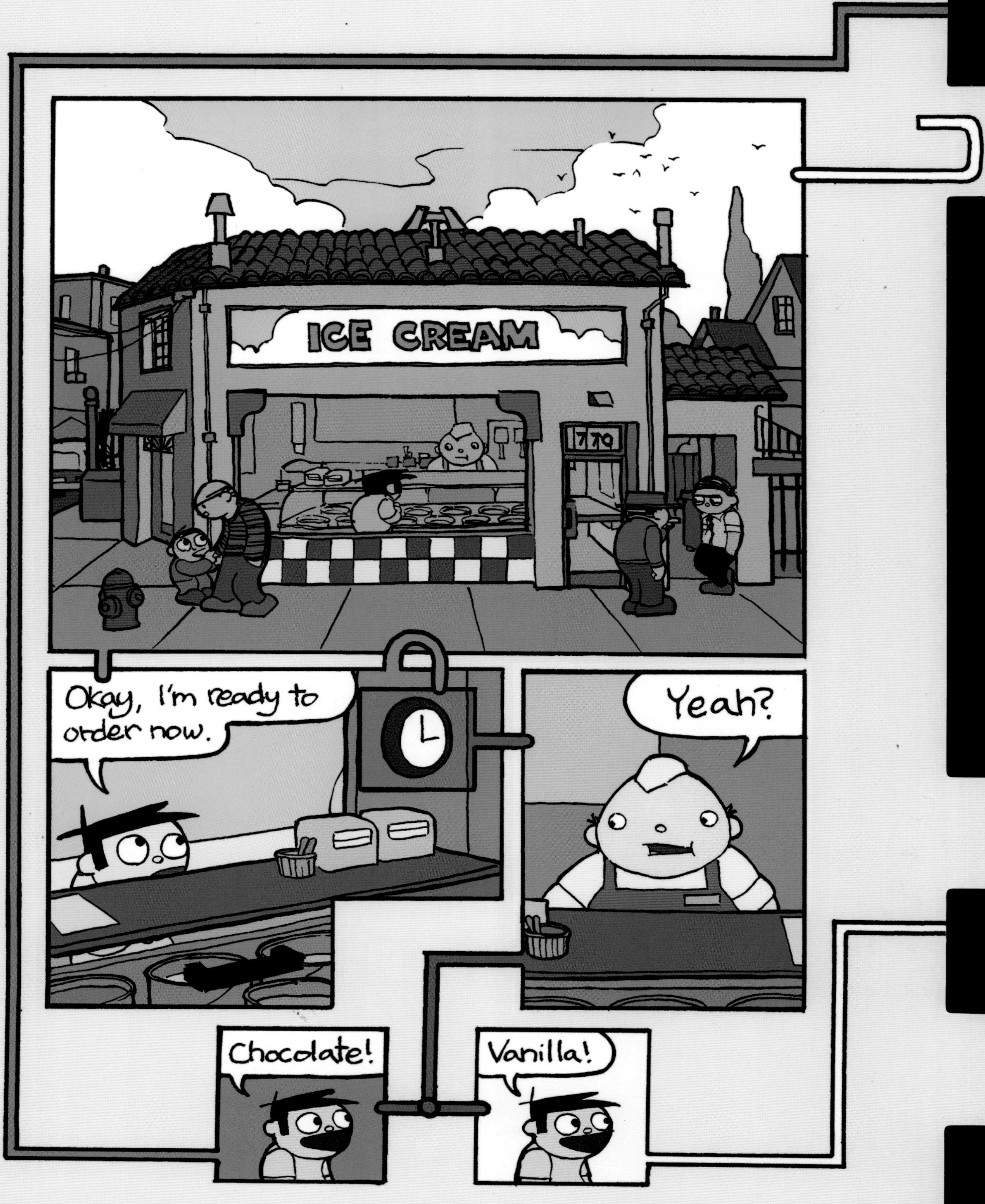
ICE CREAM
770
Okay, I'm ready to order now.
Yeah?
Chocolate!
Vanilla!

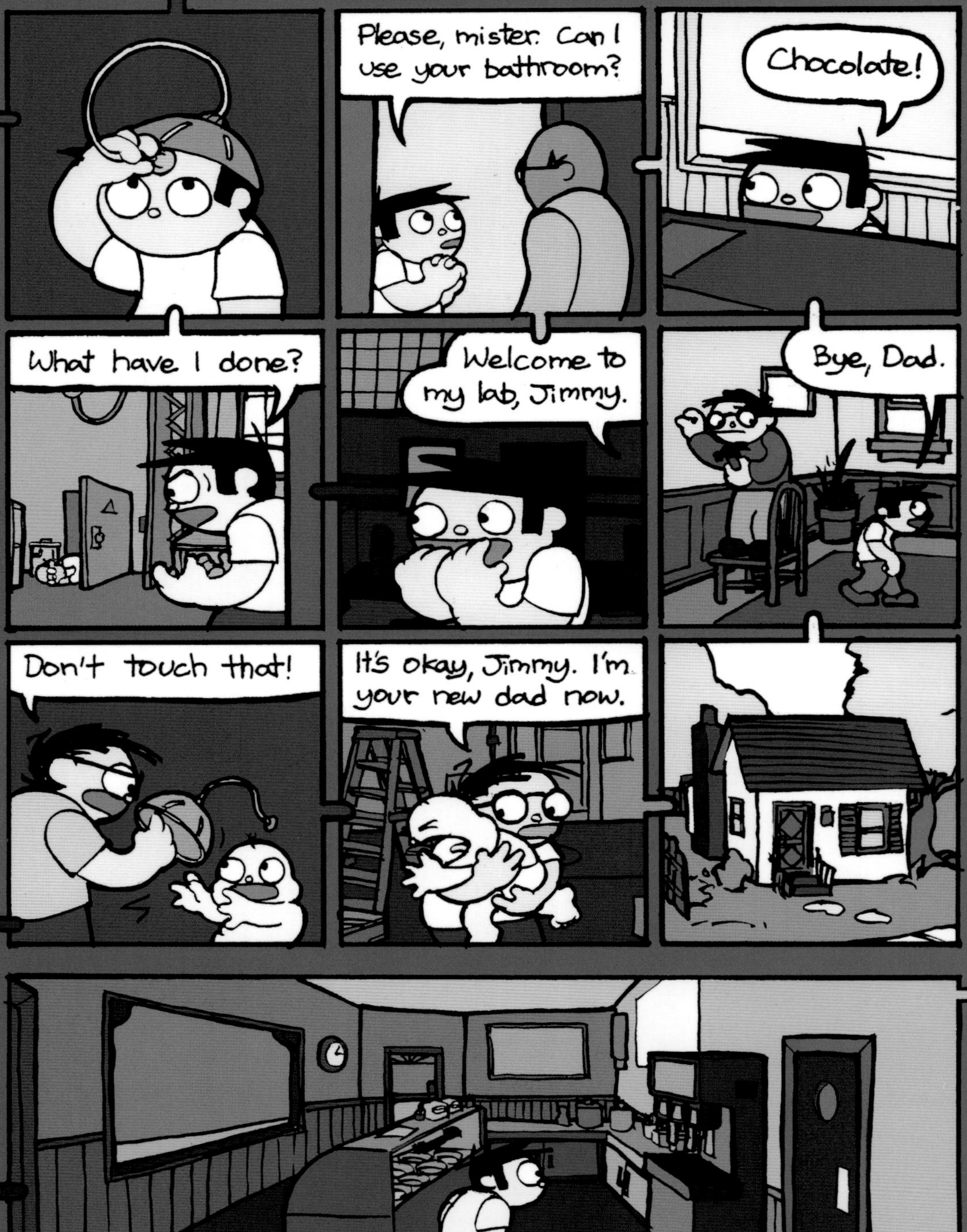
Please, mister. Can I use your bathroom?
Chocolate!
What have I done?
Welcome to my lab, Jimmy.
Bye, Dad.
Don't touch that!
It's okay, Jimmy. I'm your new dad now.

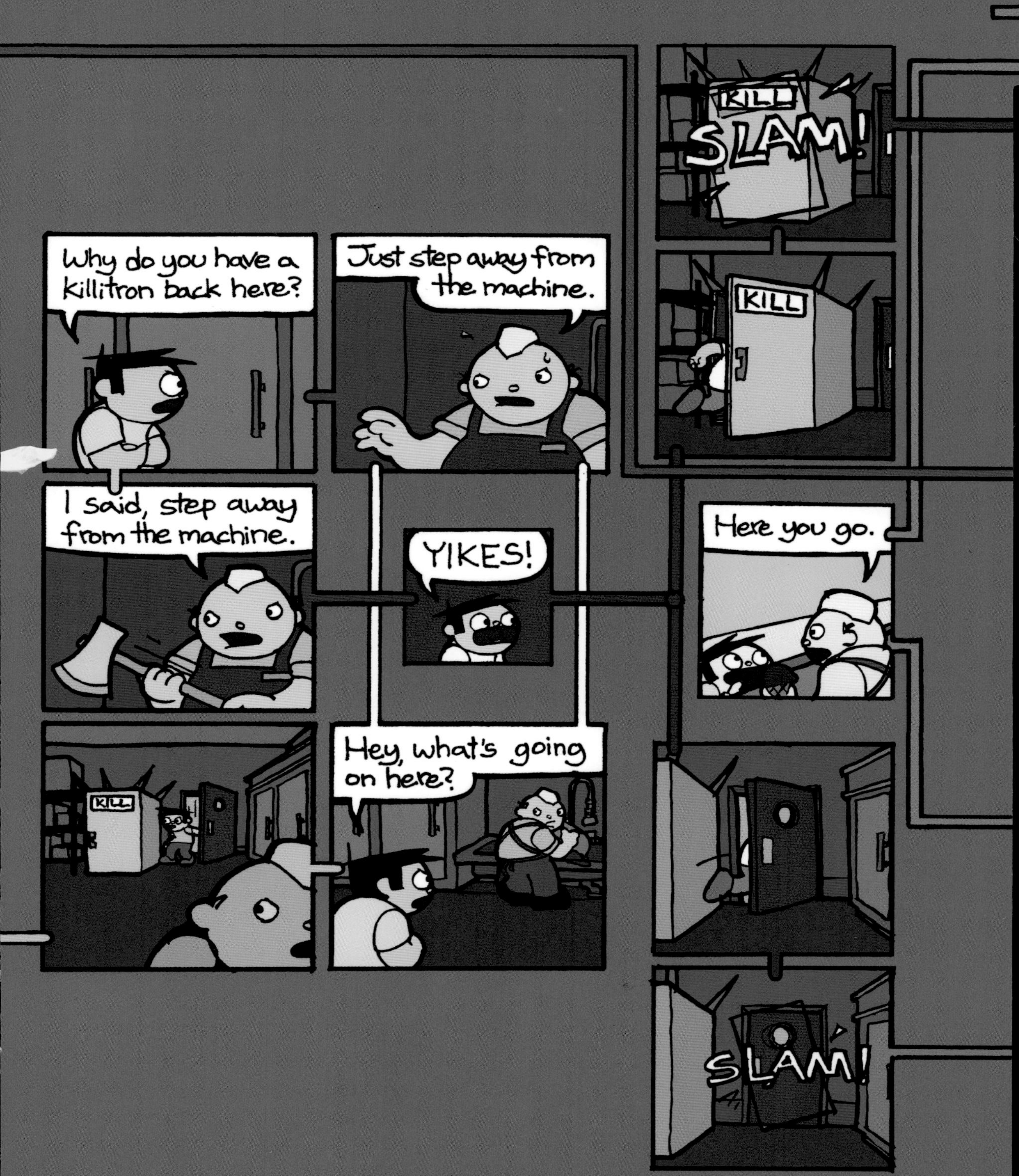
Why do you have a killitron back here?
Just step away from the machine.
I said, step away from the machine.
YIKES!
KILL
Hey, what's going on here?
SLAM!
Here you go.
KILL
KILL
SLAM!

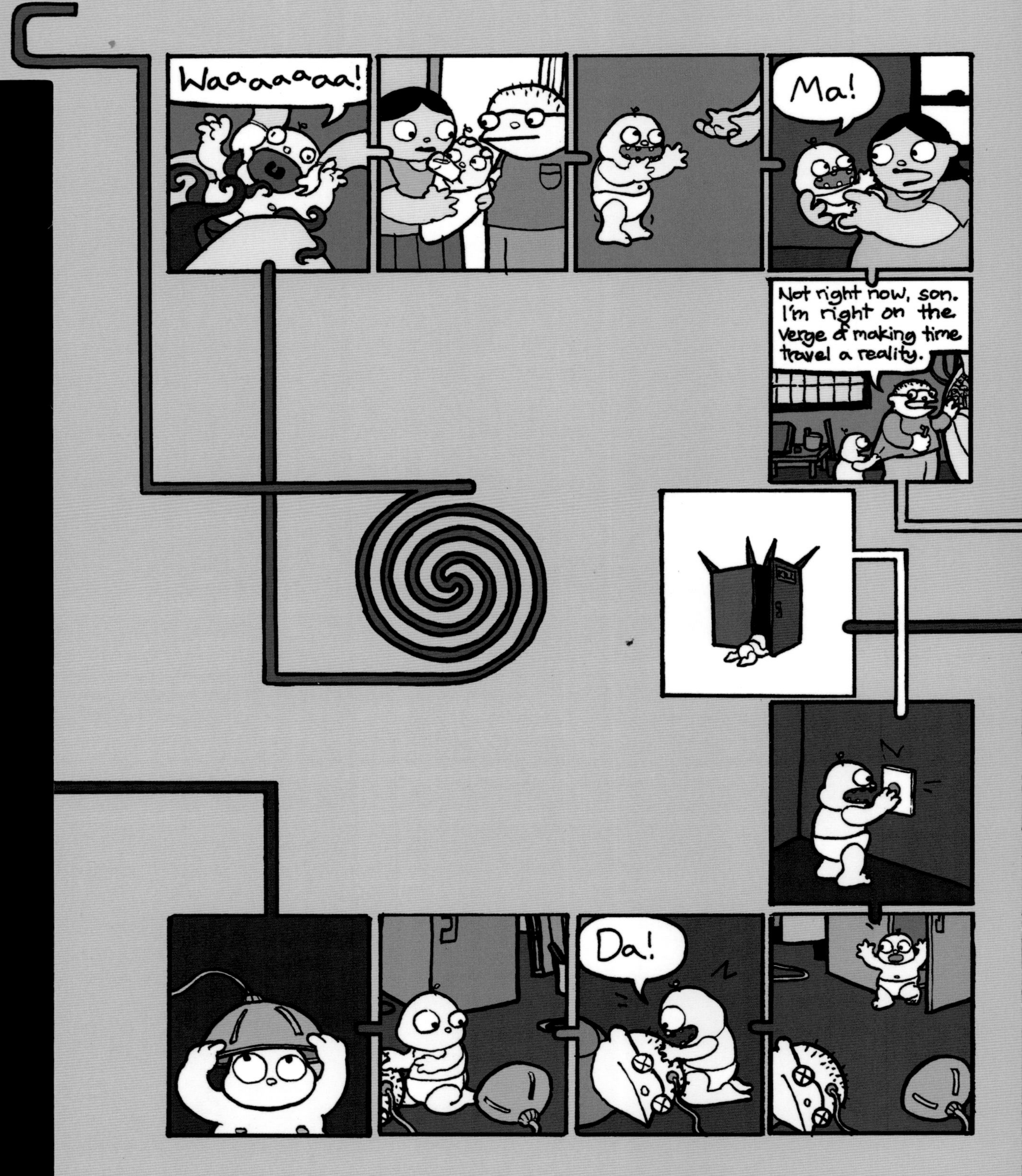

Waaaaaaa!
Ma!
Not right now, son. I'm right on the verge of making time travel a reality.
Da!

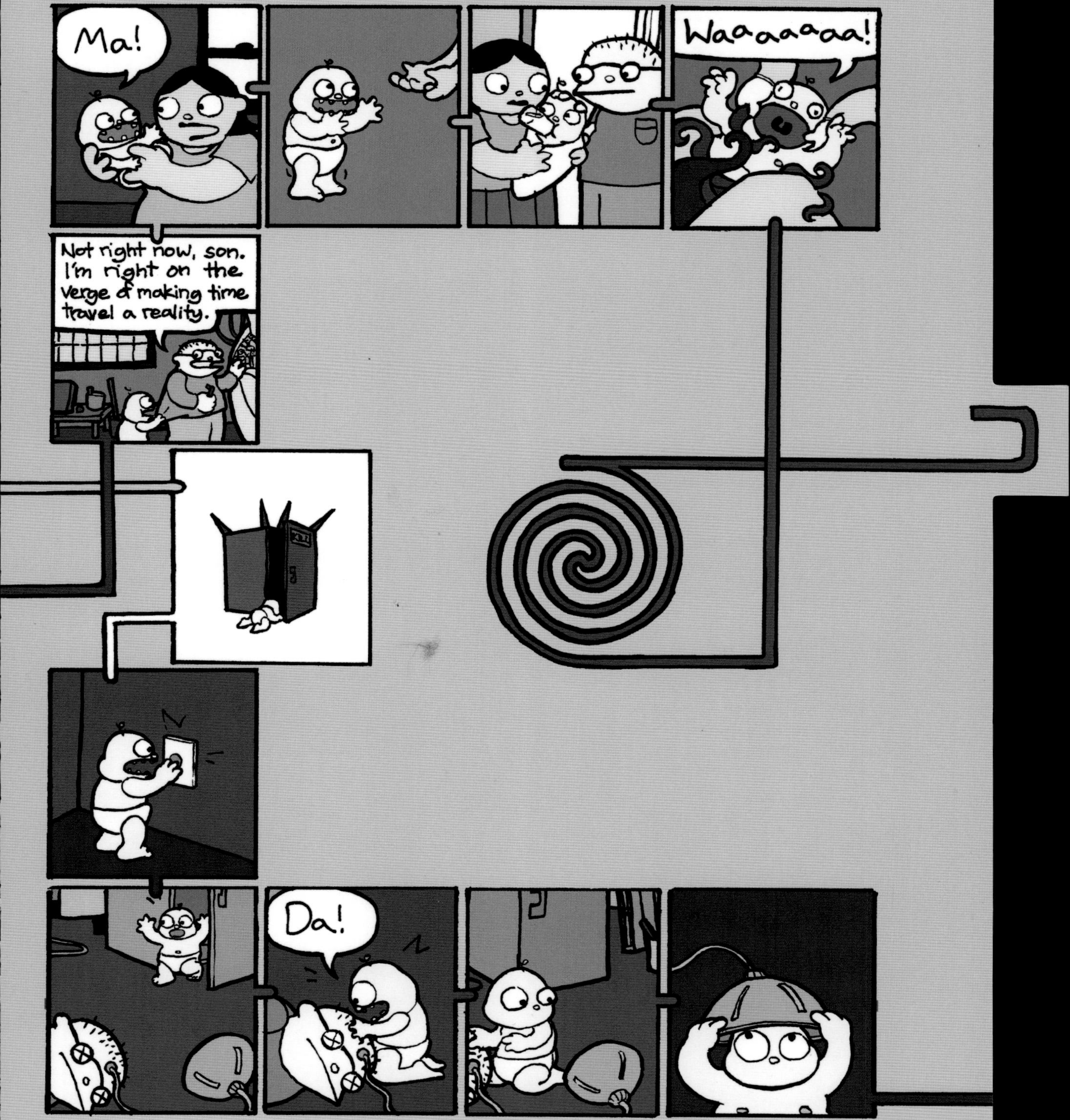
Ma!
Waaaaaaa!
Not right now, son. I'm right on the verge of making time travel a reality.
Da!

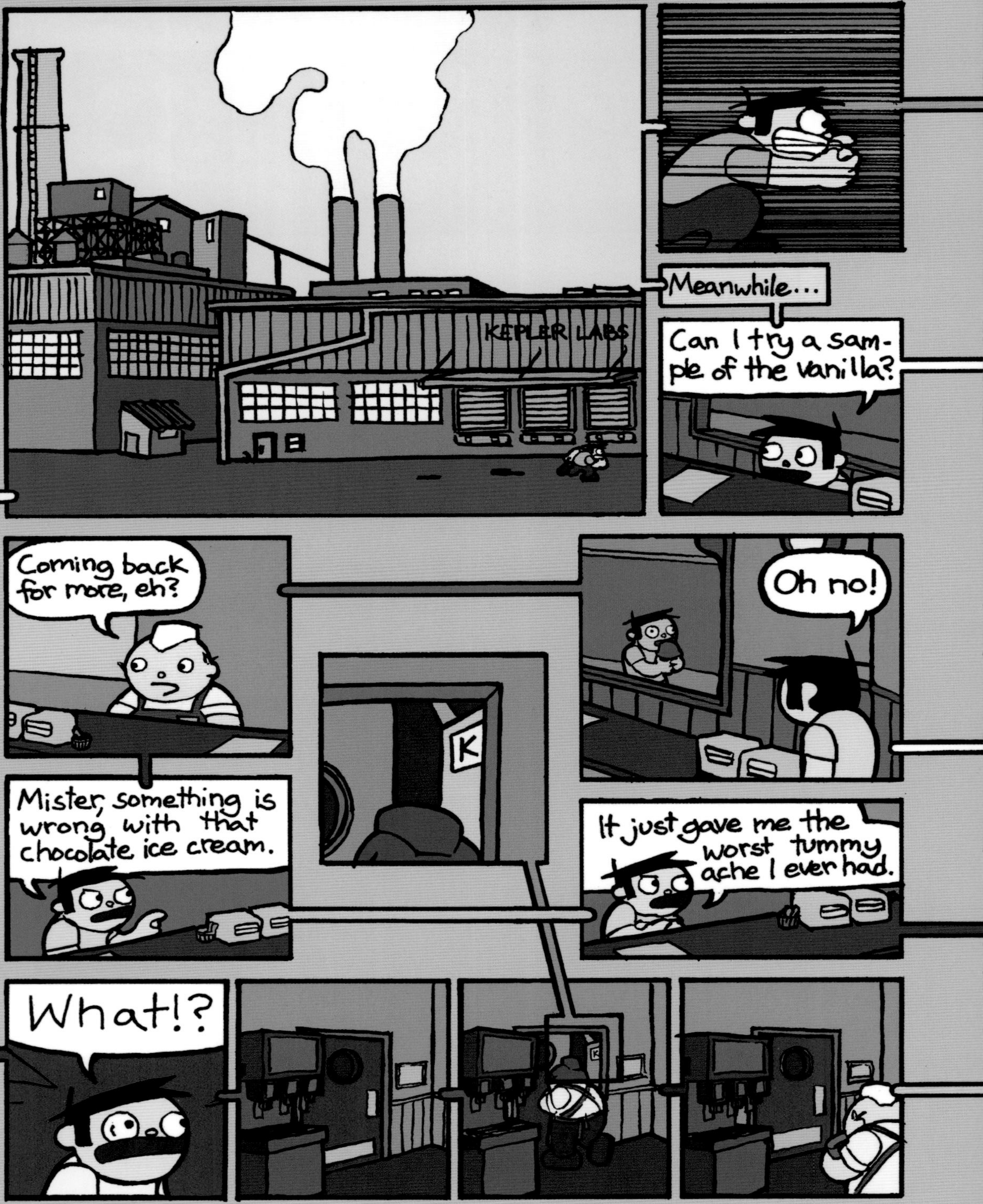
KEPLER LABS
Meanwhile...
Can I try a sample of the vanilla?
Coming back for more, eh?
Oh no!
K
Mister, something is wrong with that chocolate ice cream.
It just gave me the worst tummy ache I ever had.
What!?

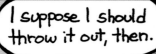
Here you go.

Don't get the chocolate!

Okay, I'm ready to order now.

Chocolate!

Where is he?

Noooo!

Yeah?

Vanilla!

I suppose I should throw it out, then.

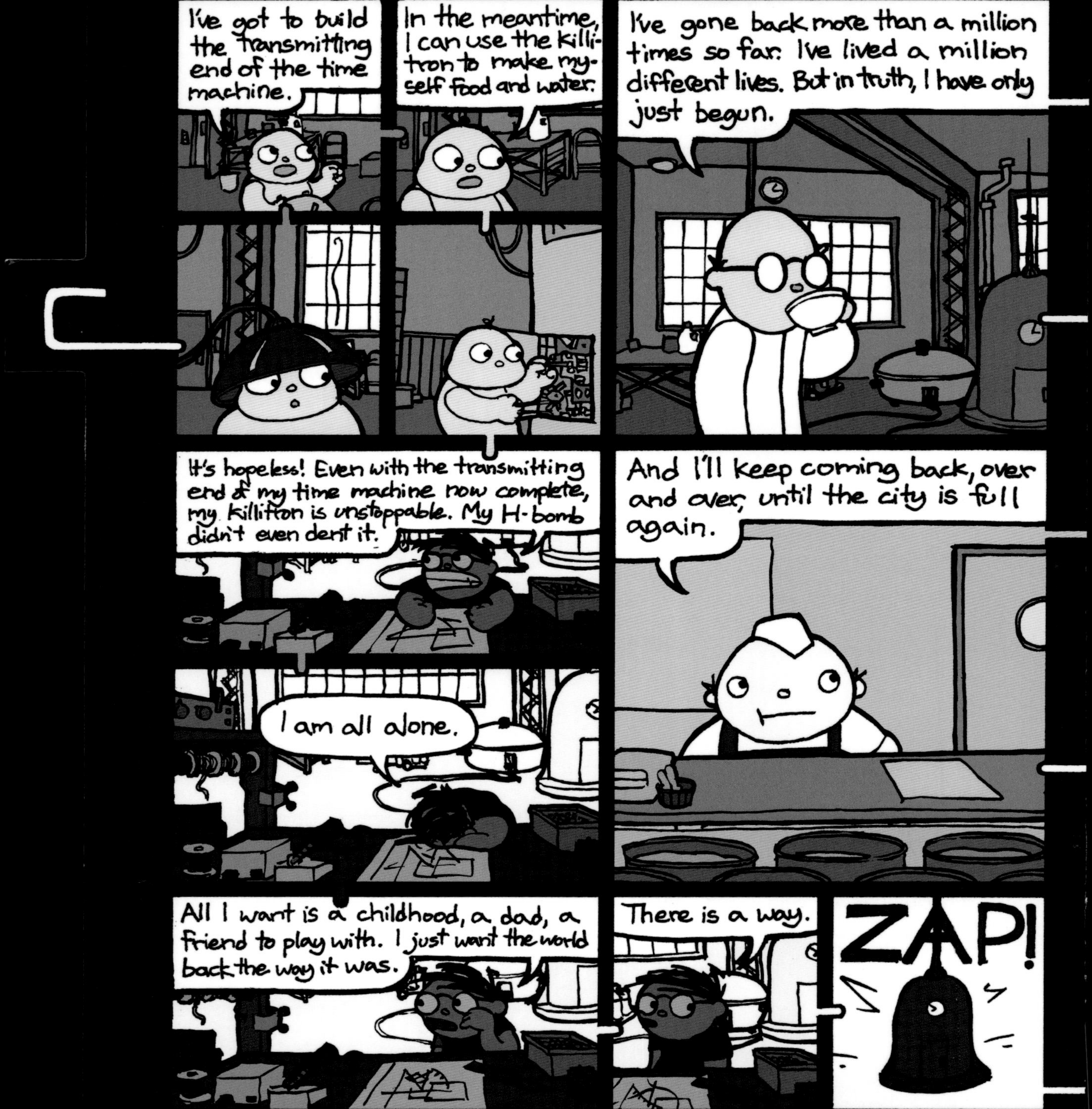
I've got to build the transmitting end of the time machine.
In the meantime, I can use the killitron to make myself food and water.
I've gone back more than a million times so far. I've lived a million different lives. But in truth, I have only just begun.
It's hopeless! Even with the transmitting end of my time machine now complete, my killitron is unstoppable. My H-bomb didn't even dent it.
I am all alone.
And I'll keep coming back, over and over, until the city is full again.
All I want is a childhood, a dad, a friend to play with. I just want the world back the way it was.
There is a way.
ZAP!

Knock! Knock!
Welcome to my lab, Jimmy.
KILL!
KILL
Until the world is full again.
KILL
Right now it's just the two of us. But when I grow old I'll return to this time again. I'll use the killitron to keep myself young, Jimmy.
It's okay, Jimmy. I'm your new dad now.
Don't touch that!

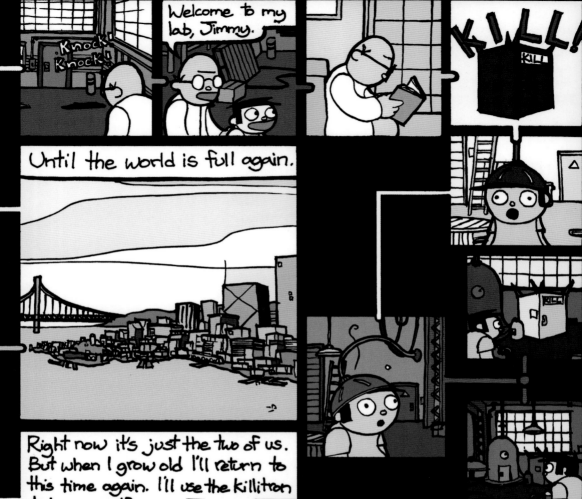

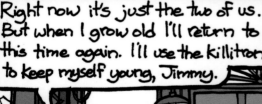

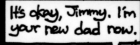

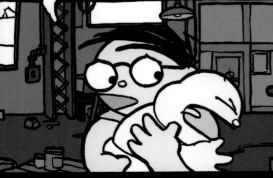

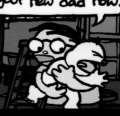

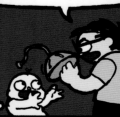

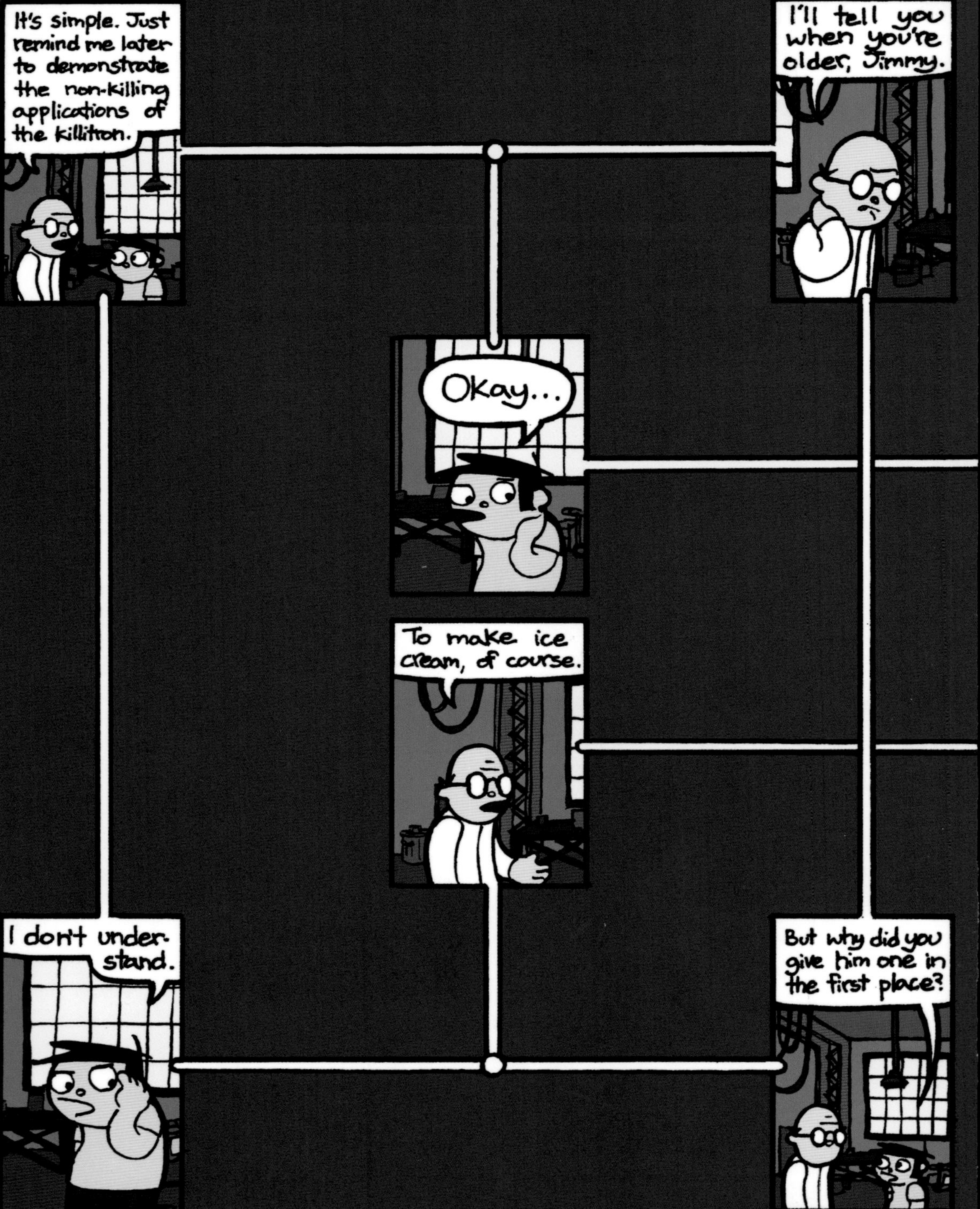
It's simple. Just remind me later to demonstrate the non-killing applications of the killitron.
I'll tell you when you're older, Jimmy.
Okay...
To make ice cream, of course.
I don't under-stand.
But why did you give him one in the first place?

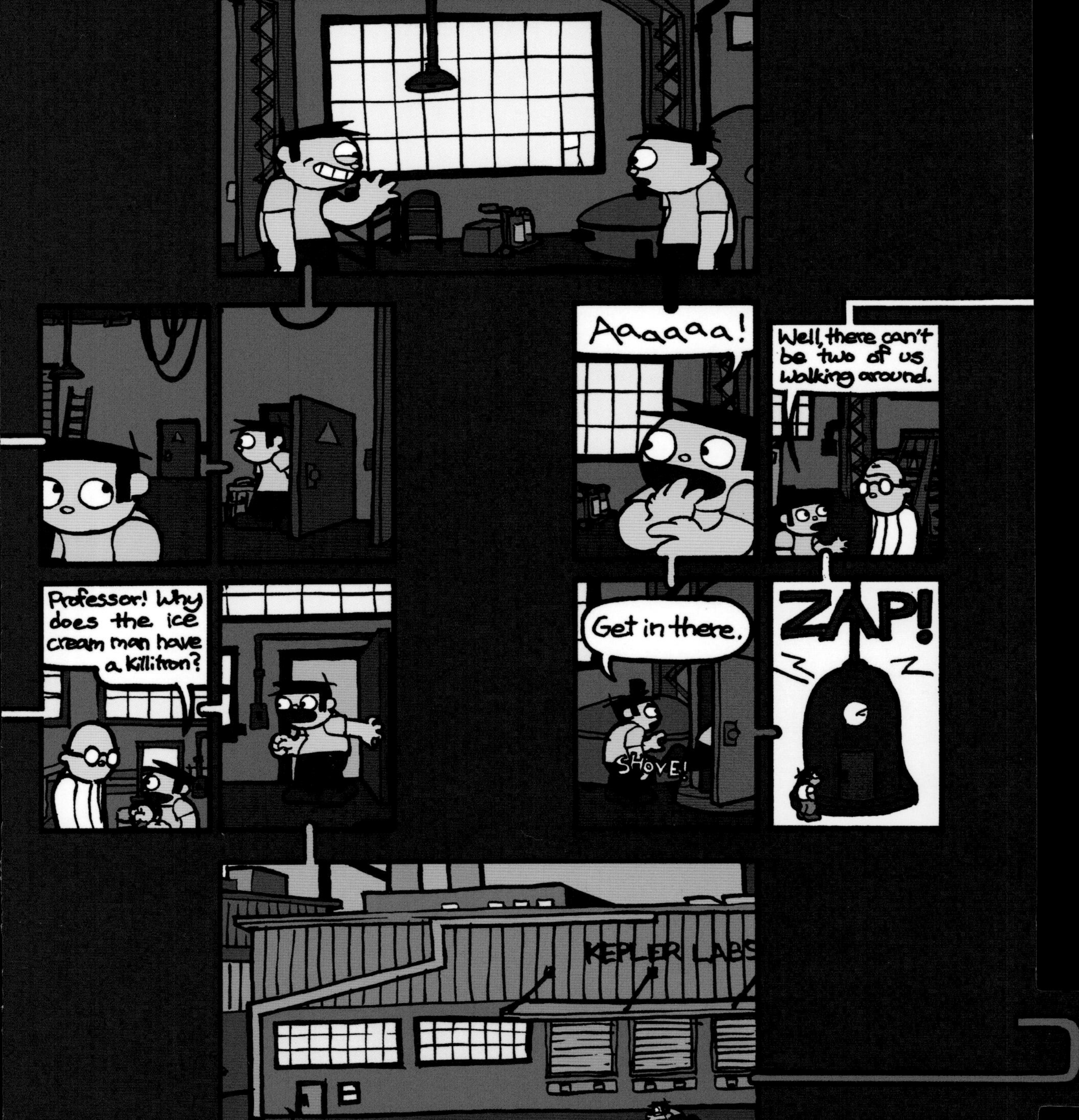
Aaaaaa!
Well, there can't be two of us walking around.
Professor! Why does the ice cream man have a Killitron?
Get in there.
SHOVE!
ZAP!
KEPLER LABS

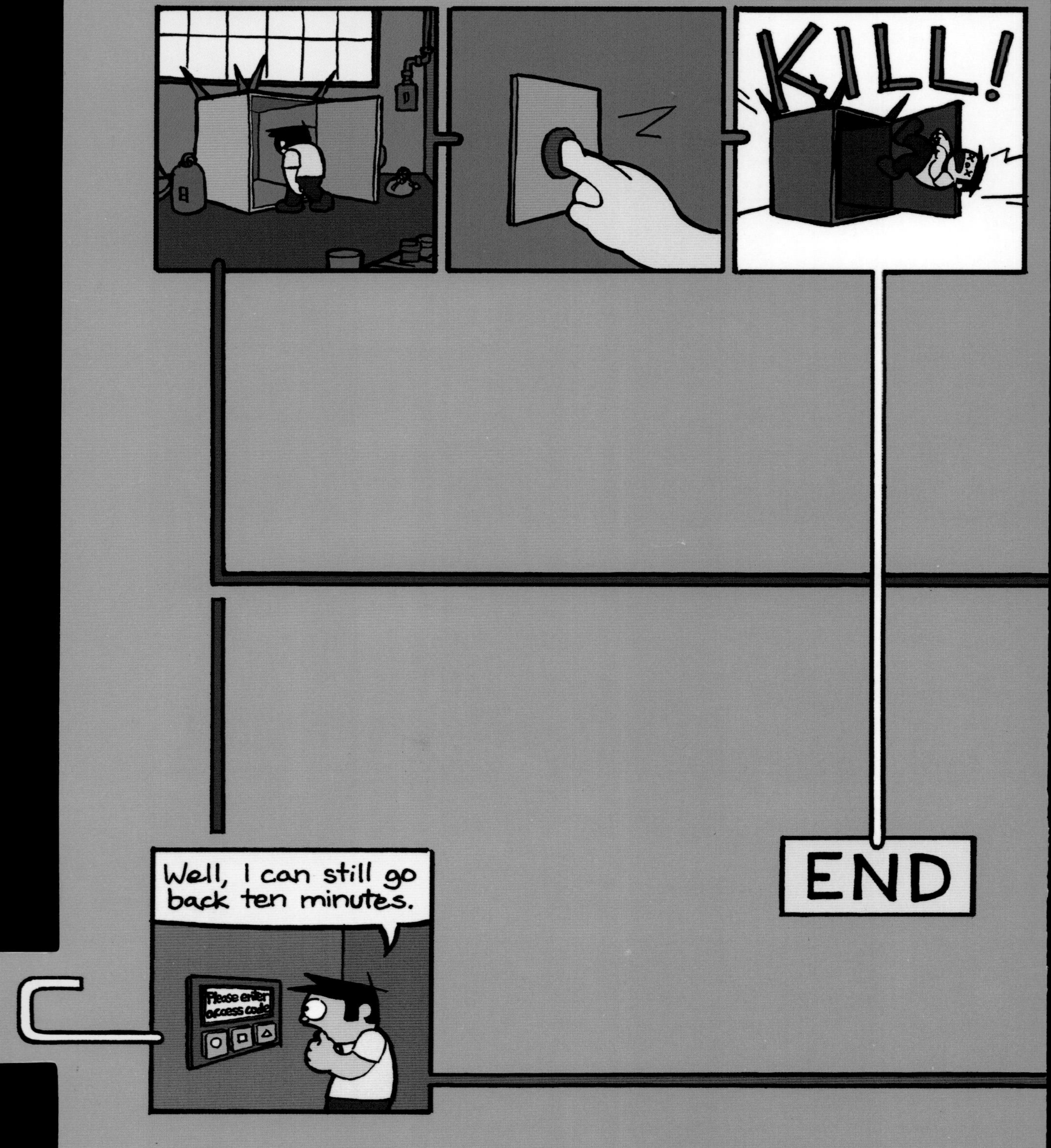
KILL!
END
Well, I can still go back ten minutes.
Please enter access code

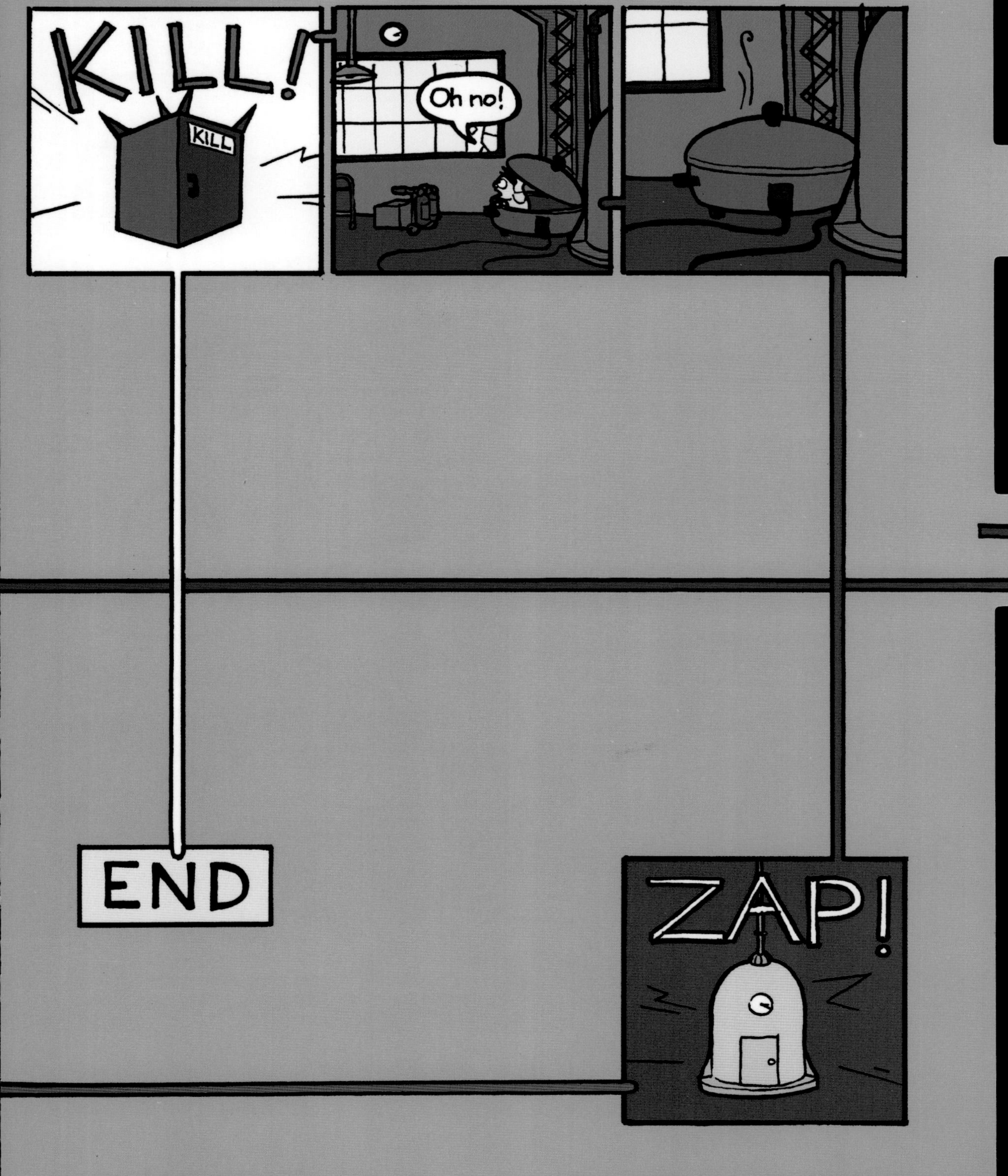
KILL!
KILL
Oh no!
END
ZAP!

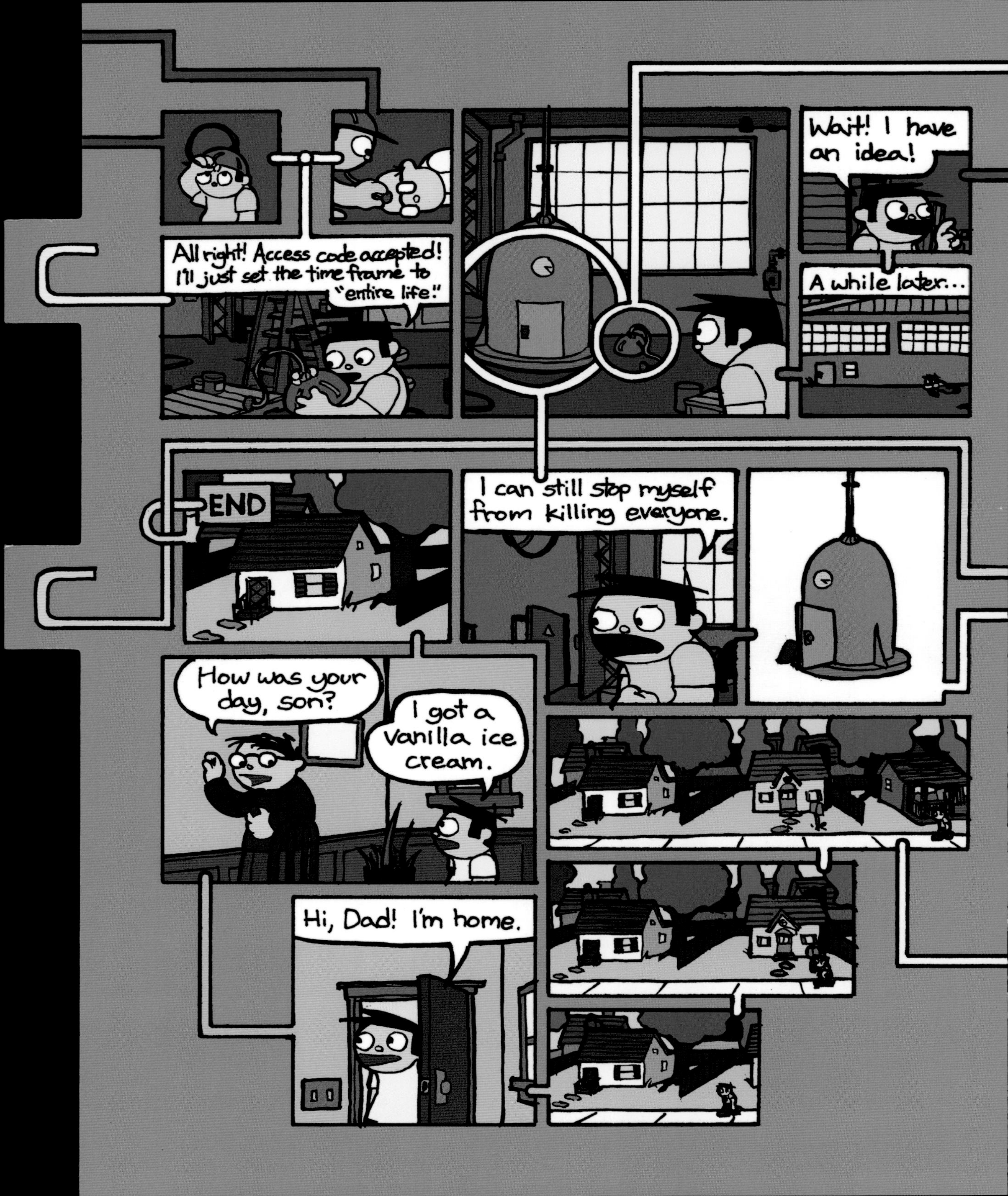
All right! Access code accepted! I'll just set the time frame to "entire life."
Wait! I have an idea!
A while later...
END
I can still stop myself from killing everyone.
How was your day, son?
I got a vanilla ice cream.
Hi, Dad! I'm home.

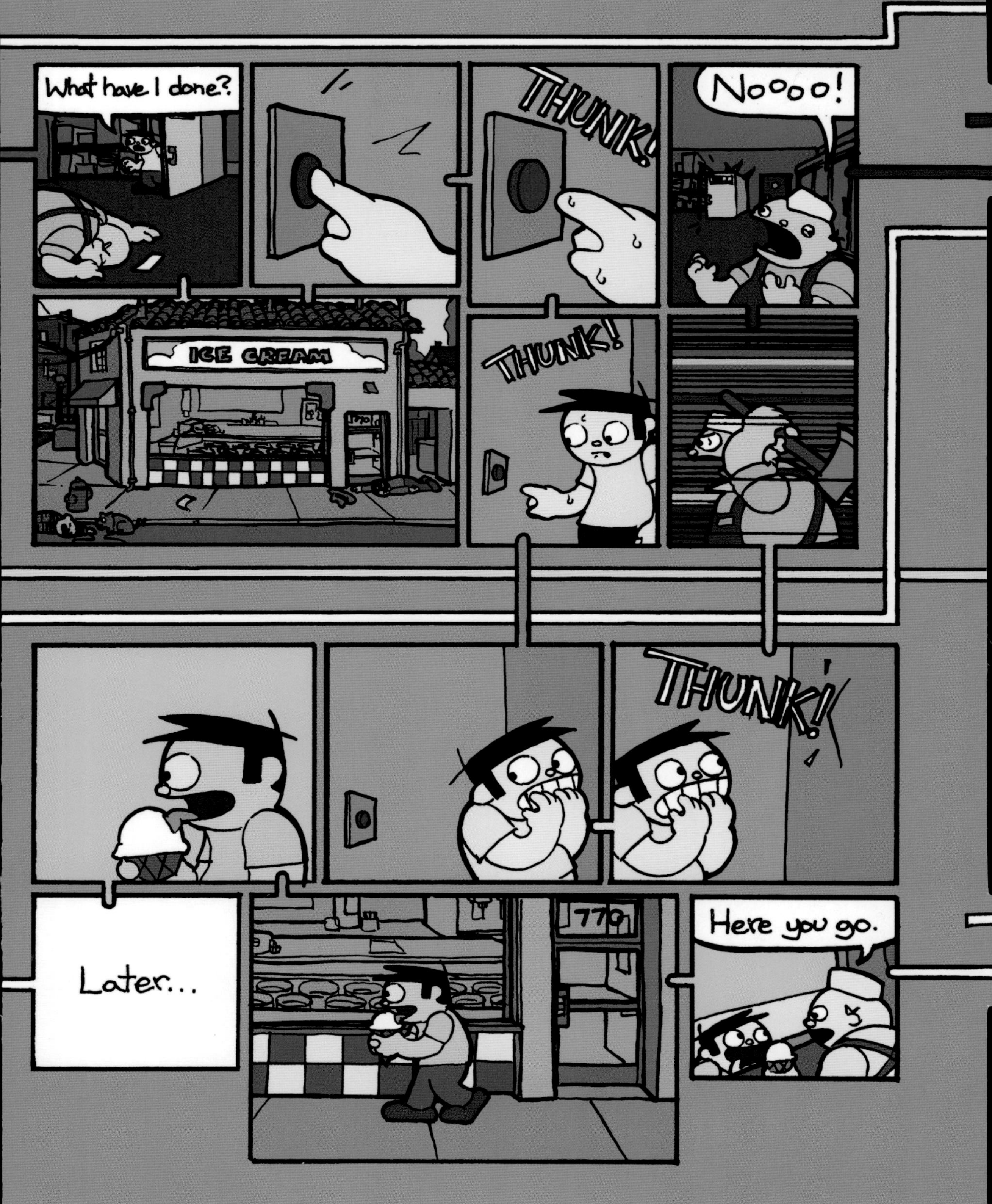
What have I done?
THUNK!
Noooo!
ICE CREAM
THUNK!
THUNK!
Later...
Here you go.

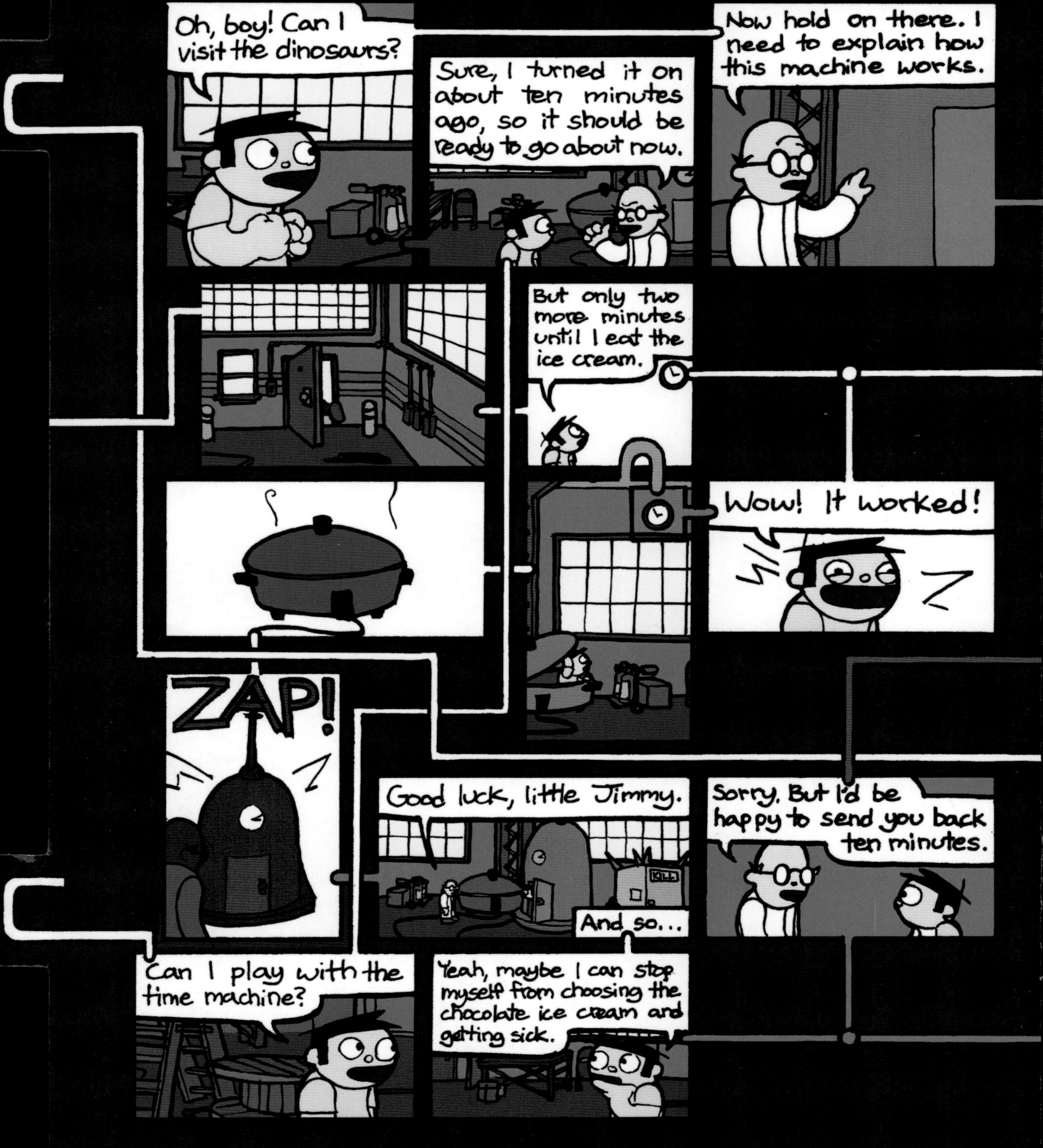
Oh, boy! Can I visit the dinosaurs?
Sure, I turned it on about ten minutes ago, so it should be ready to go about now.
Now hold on there. I need to explain how this machine works.
But only two more minutes until I eat the ice cream.
Wow! It worked!
ZAP!
Good luck, little Jimmy.
And so...
Sorry. But I'd be happy to send you back ten minutes.
Can I play with the time machine?
Yeah, maybe I can stop myself from choosing the chocolate ice cream and getting sick.

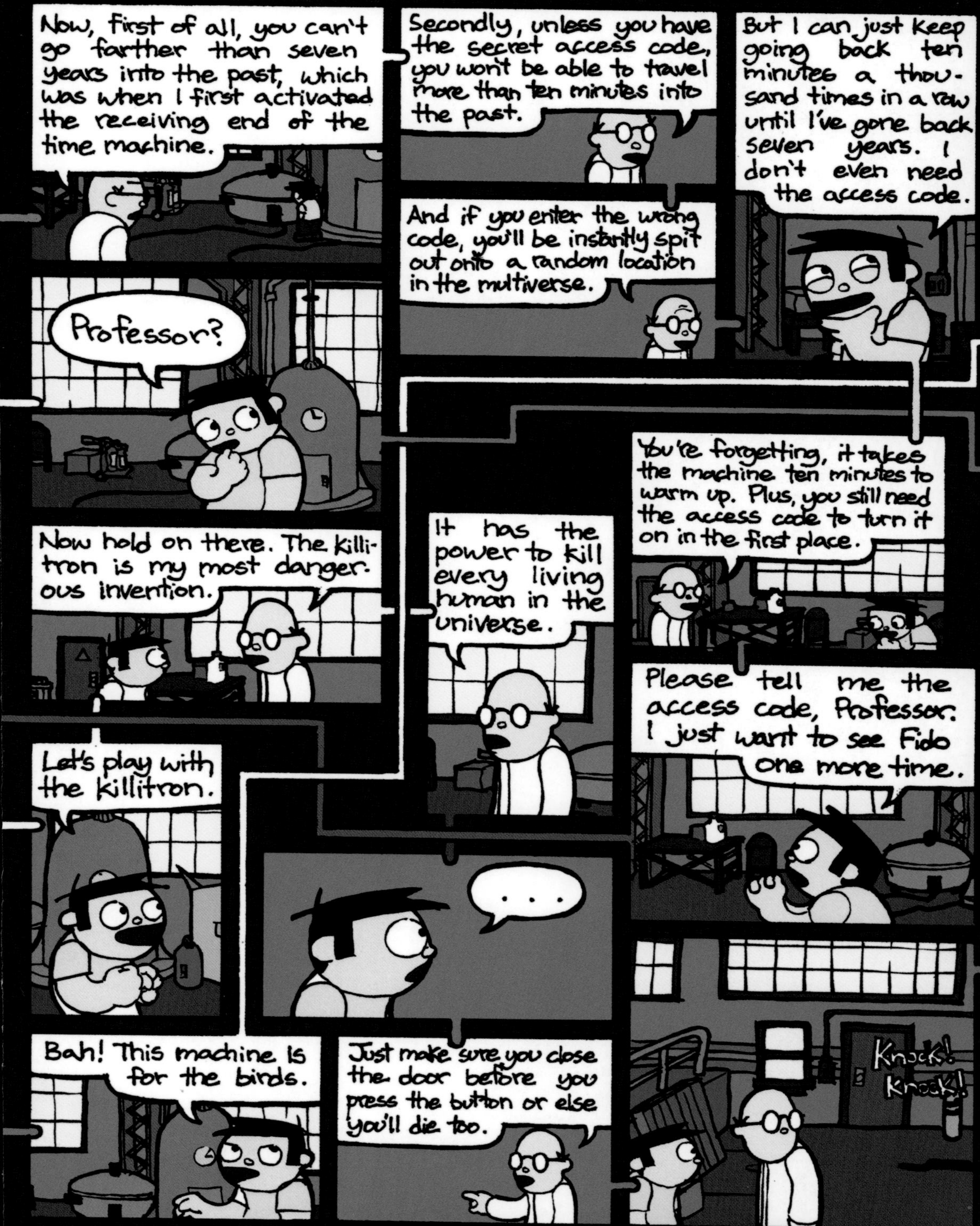
Now, first of all, you can't go farther than seven years into the past, which was when I first activated the receiving end of the time machine.
Secondly, unless you have the secret access code, you won't be able to travel more than ten minutes into the past.
And if you enter the wrong code, you'll be instantly spit out onto a random location in the multiverse.
But I can just keep going back ten minutes a thousand times in a row until I've gone back seven years. I don't even need the access code.
Professor?
You're forgetting, it takes the machine ten minutes to warm up. Plus, you still need the access code to turn it on in the first place.
Now hold on there. The killitron is my most dangerous invention.
It has the power to kill every living human in the universe.
Please tell me the access code, Professor. I just want to see Fido one more time.
Let's play with the killitron.
. . .
Bah! This machine is for the birds.
Just make sure you close the door before you press the button or else you'll die too.
Knock! Knock!

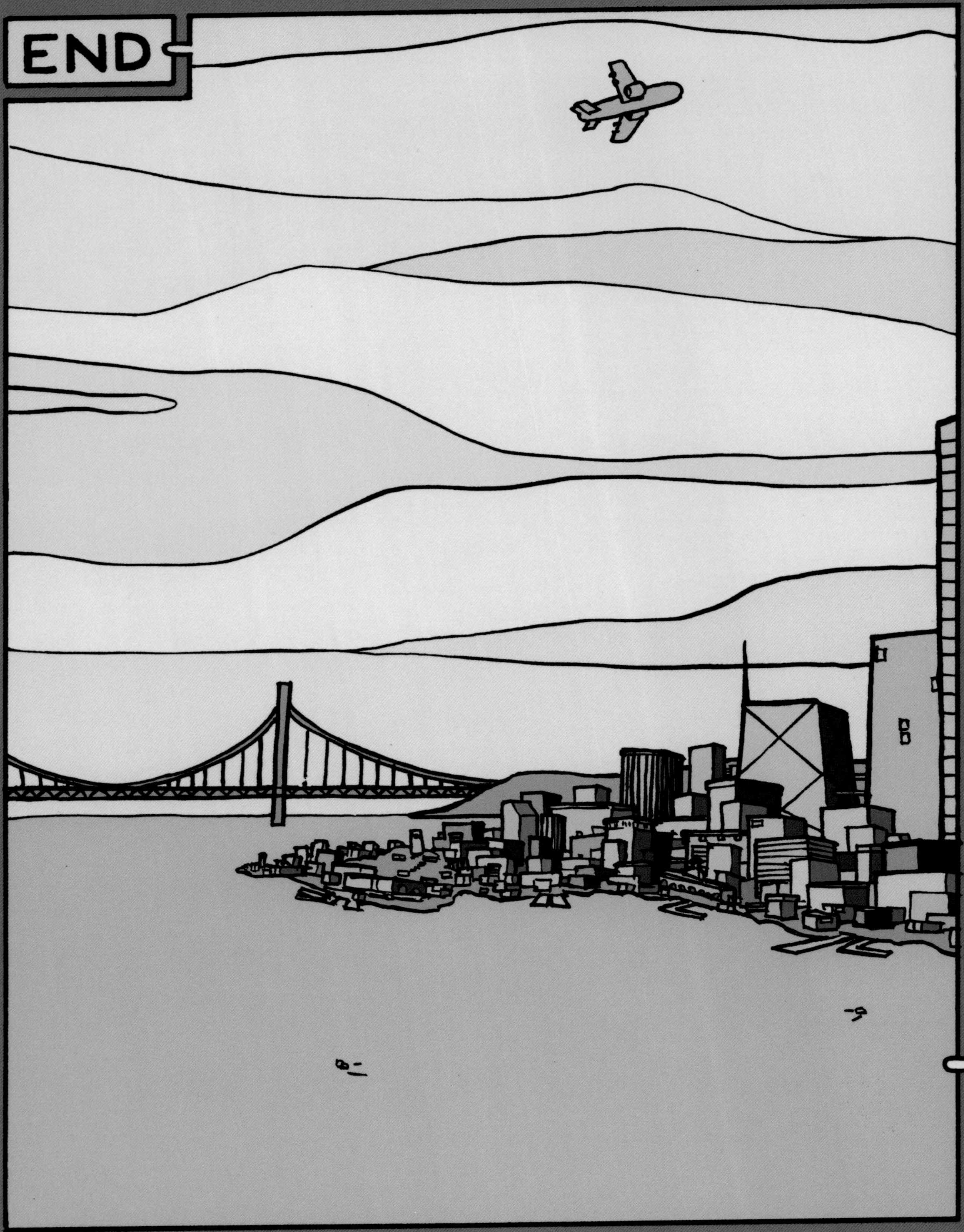
END

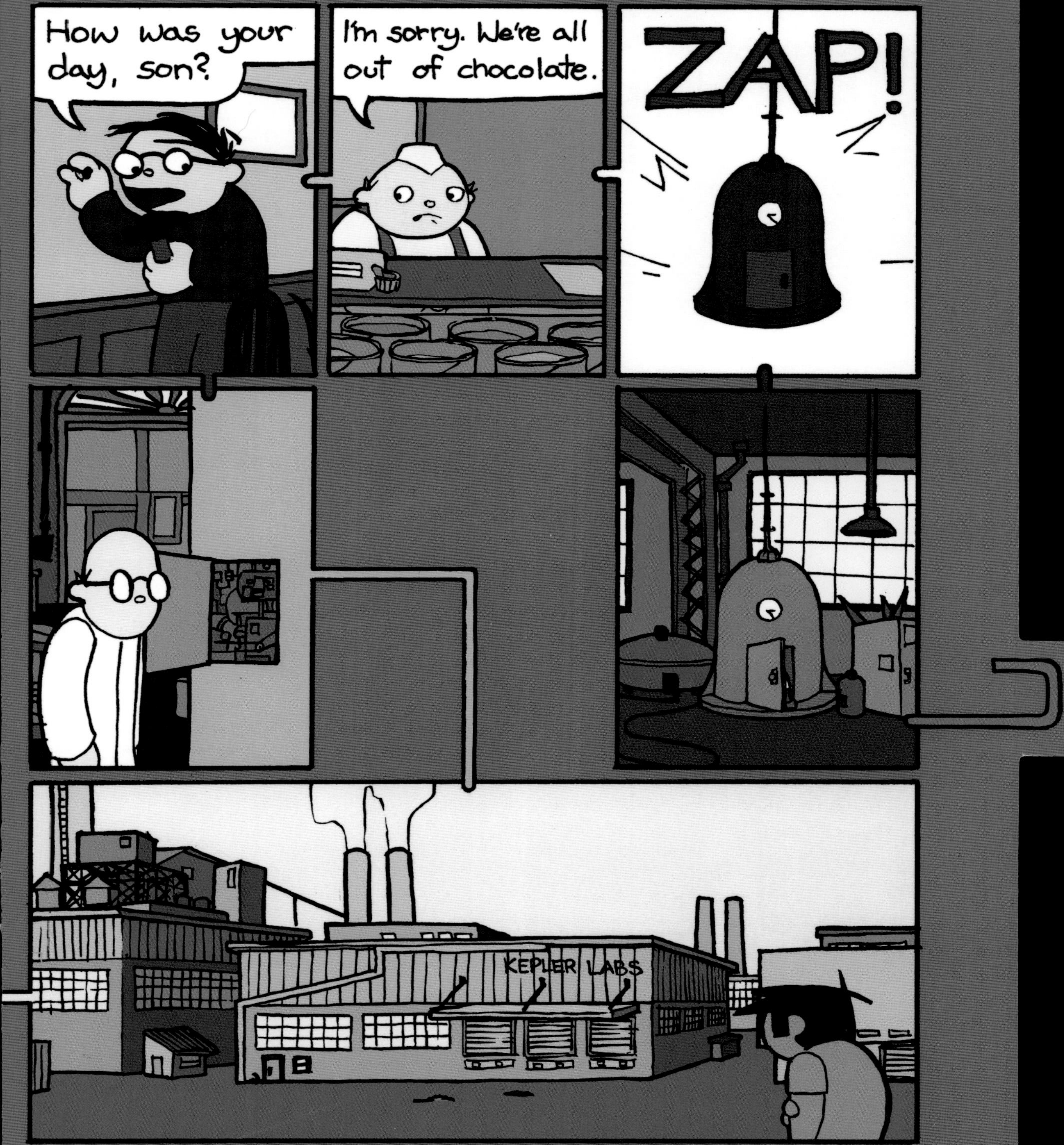
How was your day, son?
I'm sorry. We're all out of chocolate.
ZAP!
KEPLER LABS

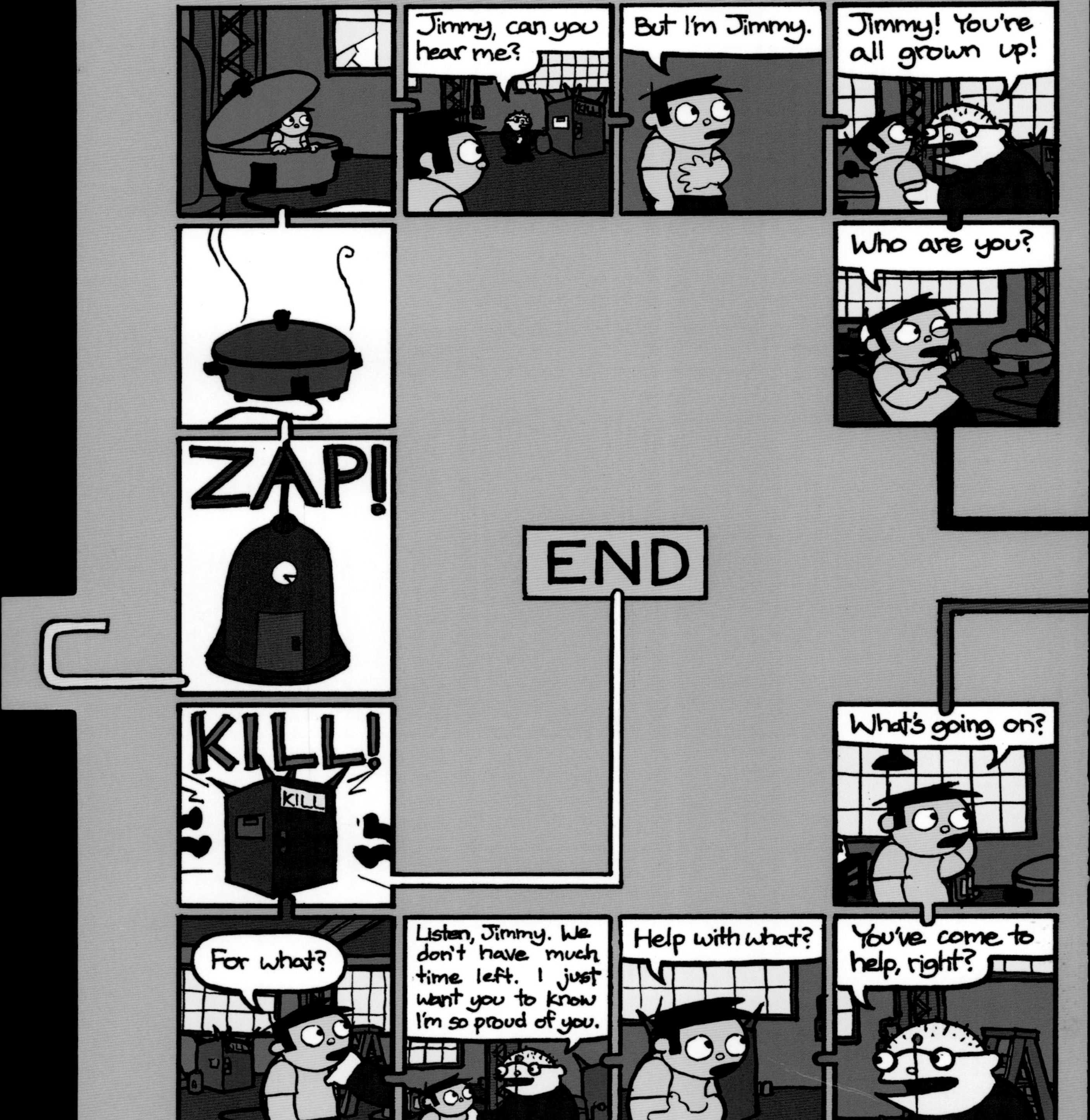
Jimmy, can you hear me?
But I'm Jimmy.
Jimmy! You're all grown up!
Who are you?
ZAP!
END
KILL!
KILL
What's going on?
For what?
Listen, Jimmy. We don't have much time left. I just want you to know I'm so proud of you.
Help with what?
You've come to help, right?

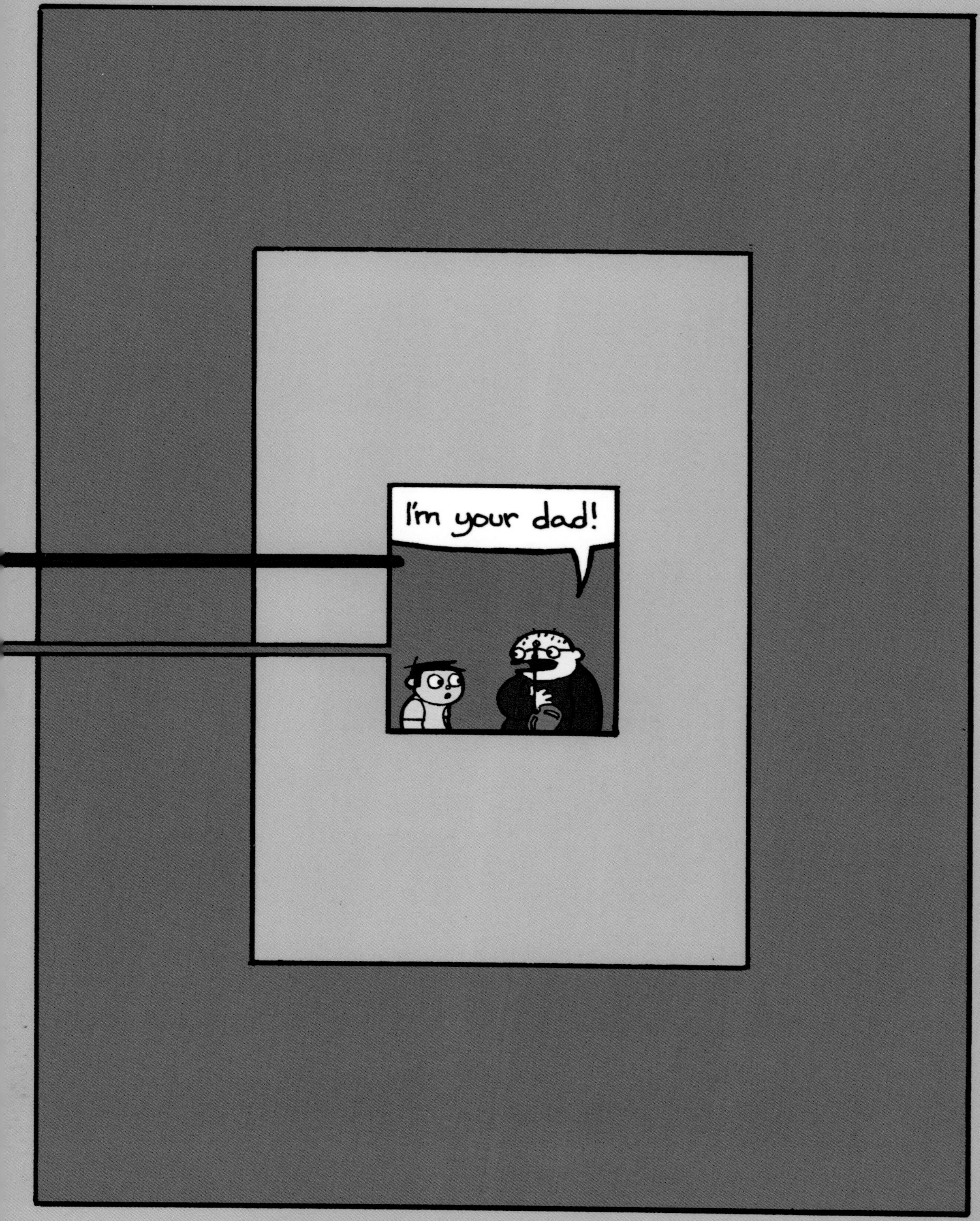
I'm your dad!

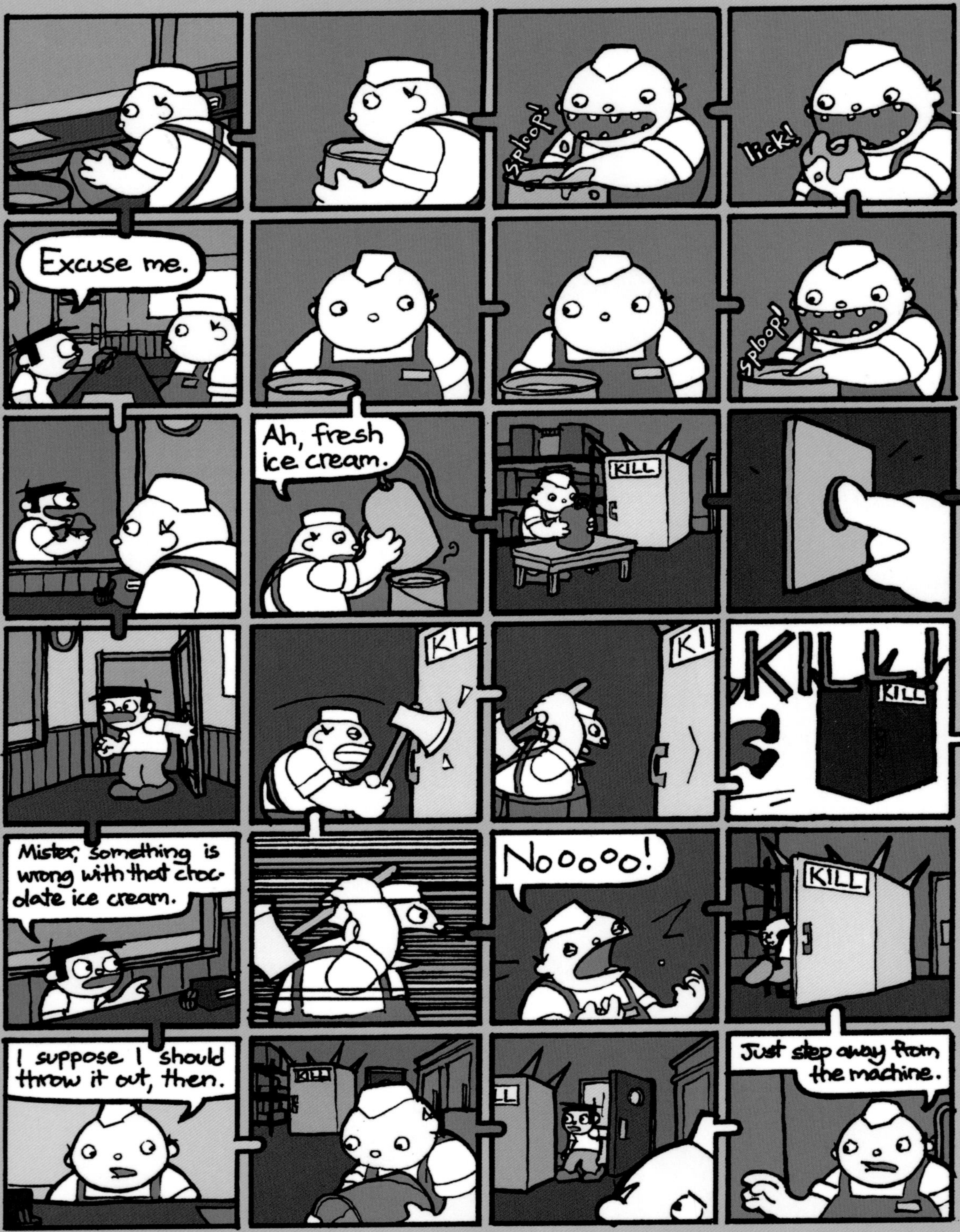
sploop!
lick!
Excuse me.
sploop!
Ah, fresh ice cream.
KILL
KILL
KILL
KILL!
KILL
Mister, something is wrong with that chocolate ice cream.
Nooooo!
KILL
I suppose I should throw it out, then.
Just step away from the machine.

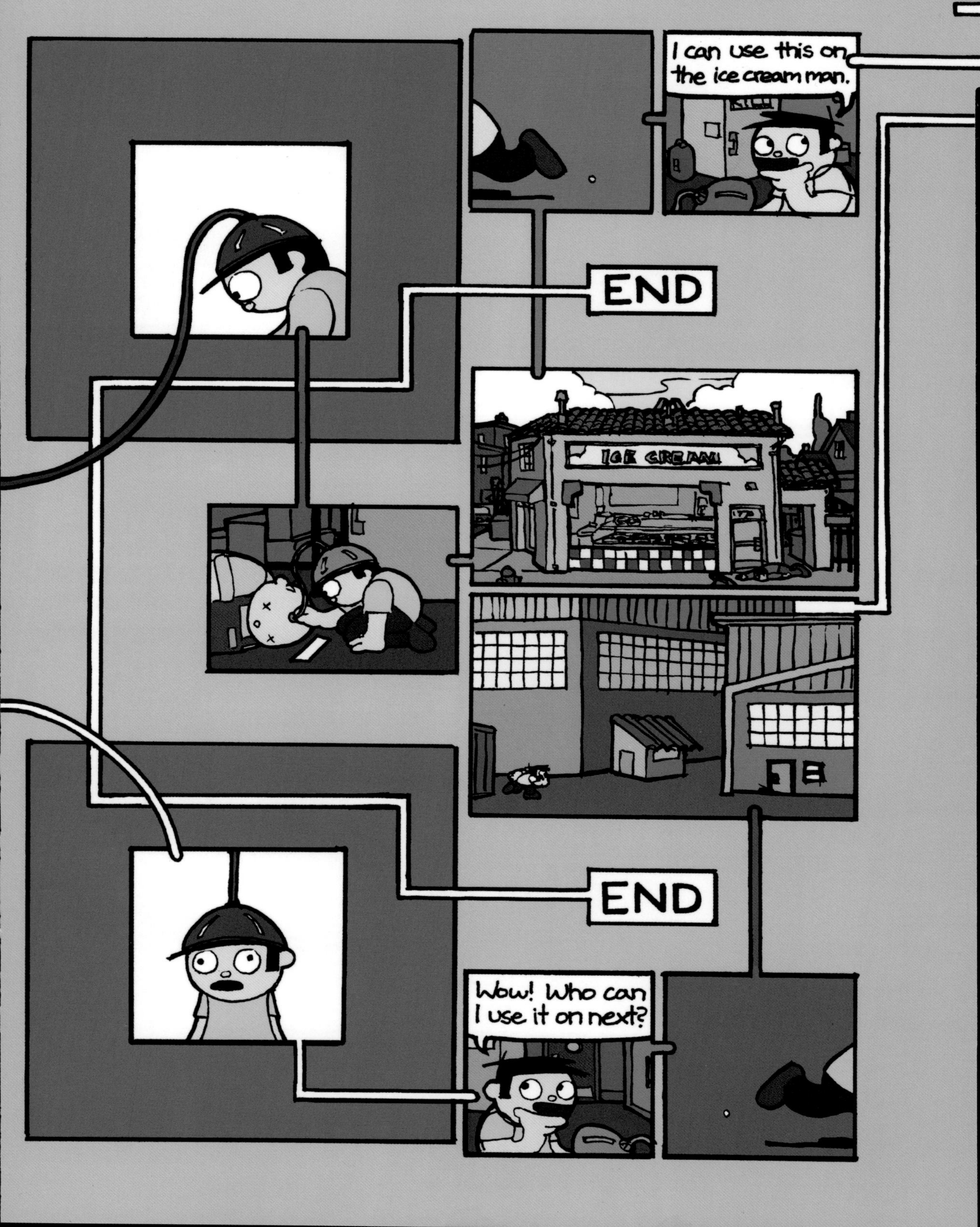
I can use this on the ice cream man.
END
ICE CREAM
END
Wow! Who can I use it on next?

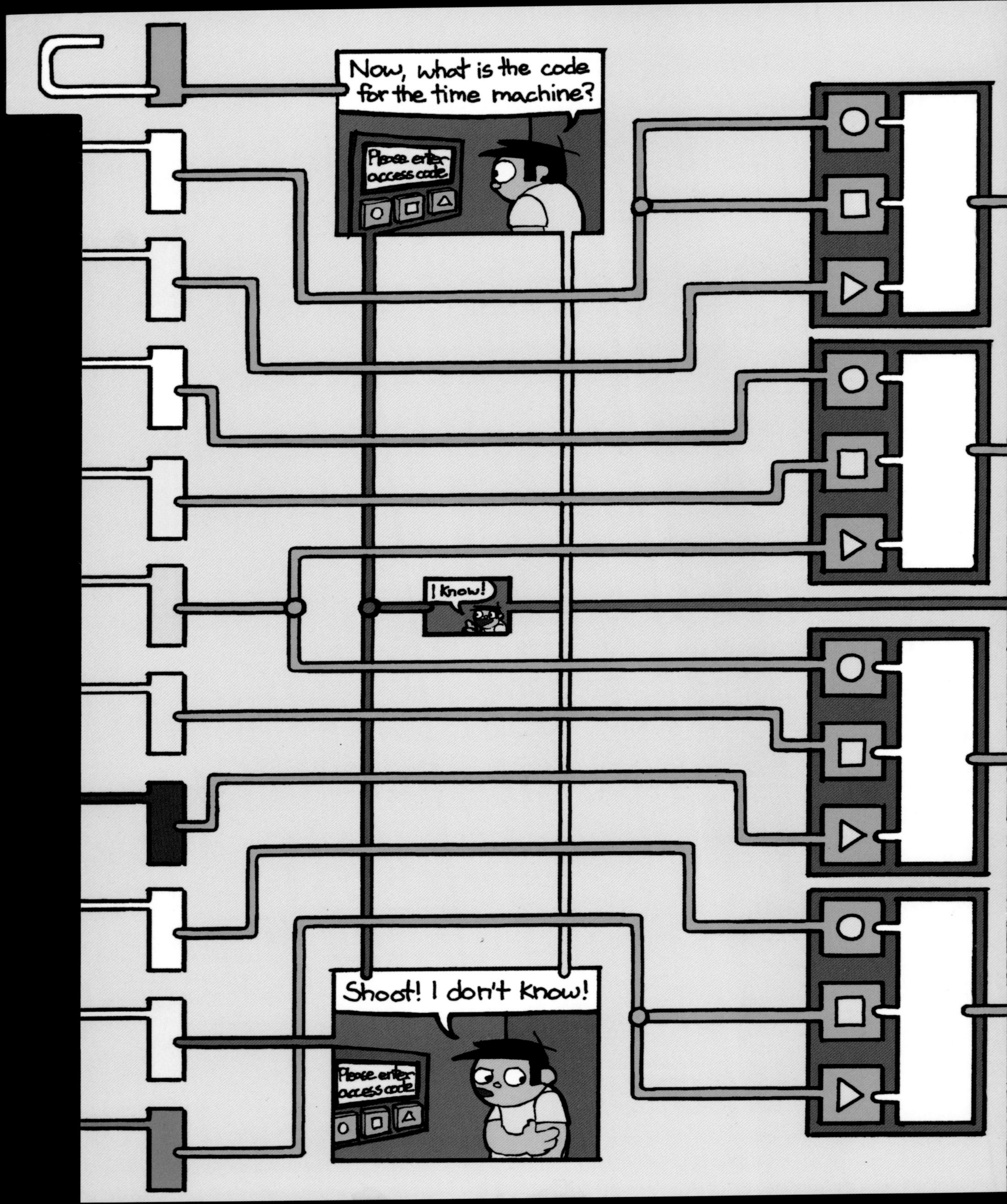
Now, what is the code for the time machine?
Please enter access code
I know!
Shoot! I don't know!
Please enter access code

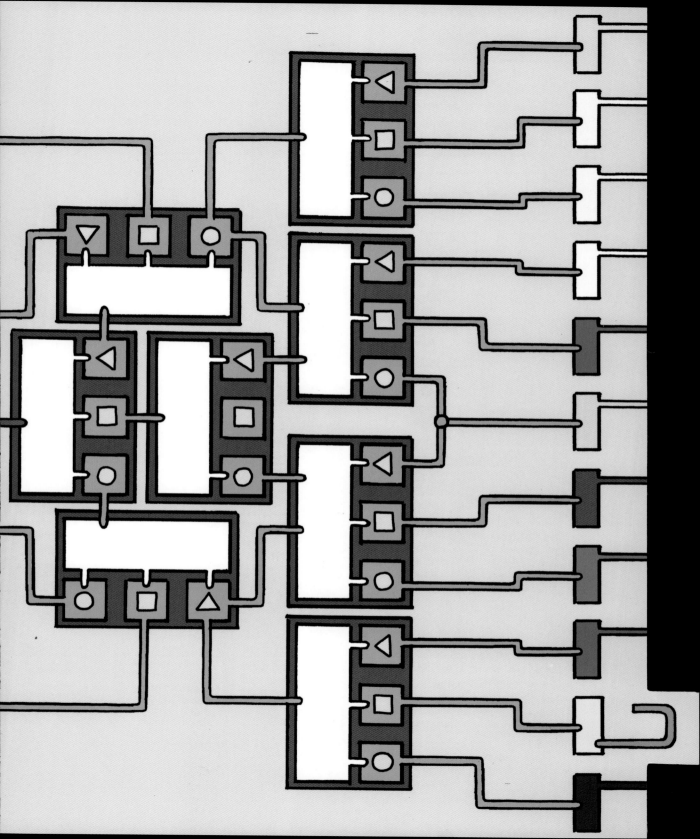

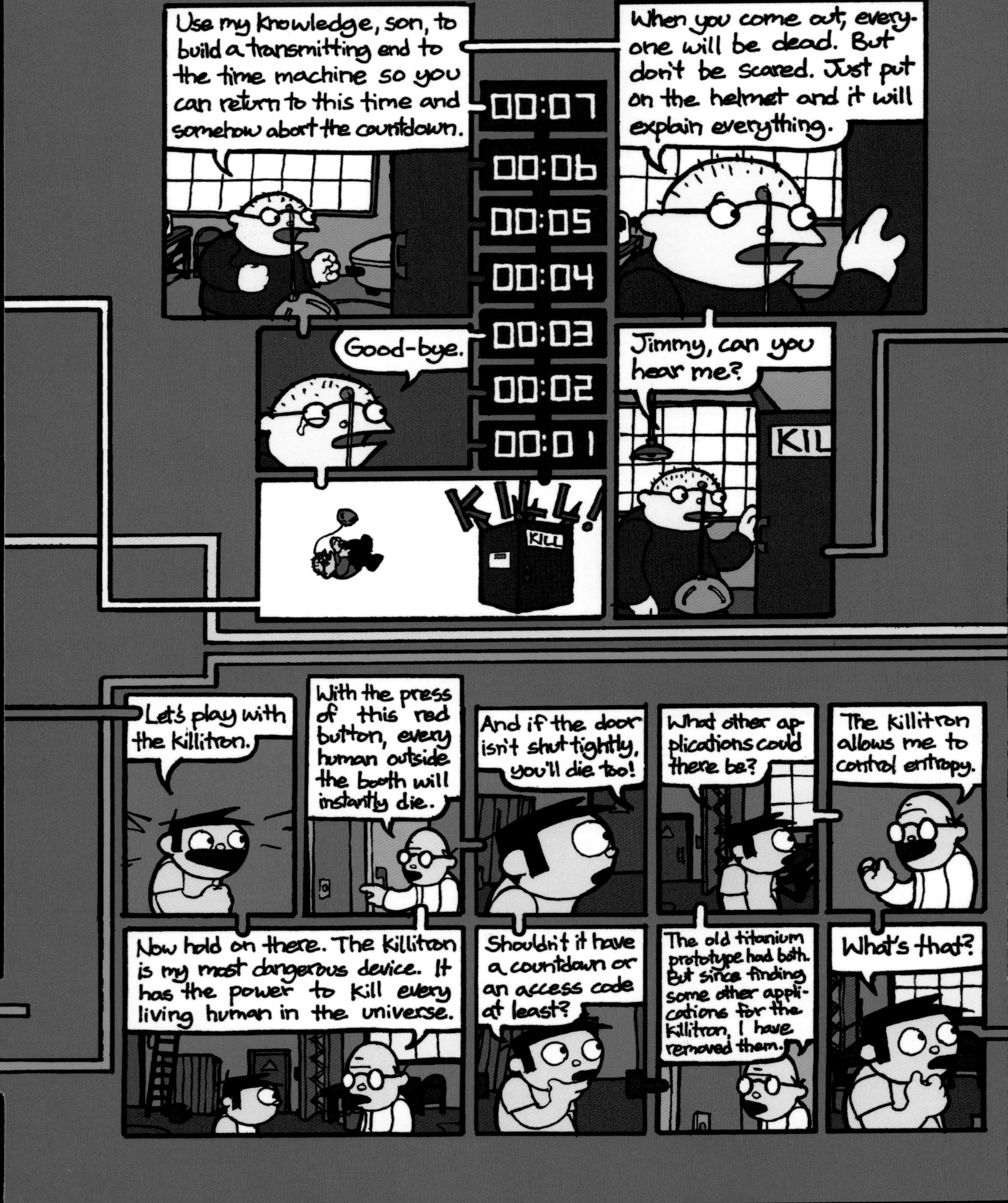
Use my knowledge, son, to build a transmitting end to the time machine so you can return to this time and somehow abort the countdown.
00:07
00:06
00:05
00:04
When you come out, every-one will be dead. But don't be scared. Just put on the helmet and it will explain everything.
Good-bye.
00:03
00:02
00:01
KILL!
KILL
Jimmy, can you hear me?
KIL
Let's play with the killitron.
With the press of this red button, every human outside the booth will instantly die.
And if the door isn't shut tightly, you'll die too!
What other ap-plications could there be?
The killitron allows me to control entropy.
Now hold on there. The killitron is my most dangerous device. It has the power to kill every living human in the universe.
Shouldn't it have a countdown or an access code at least?
The old titanium prototype had both. But since finding some other appli-cations for the killitron, I have removed them.
What's that?

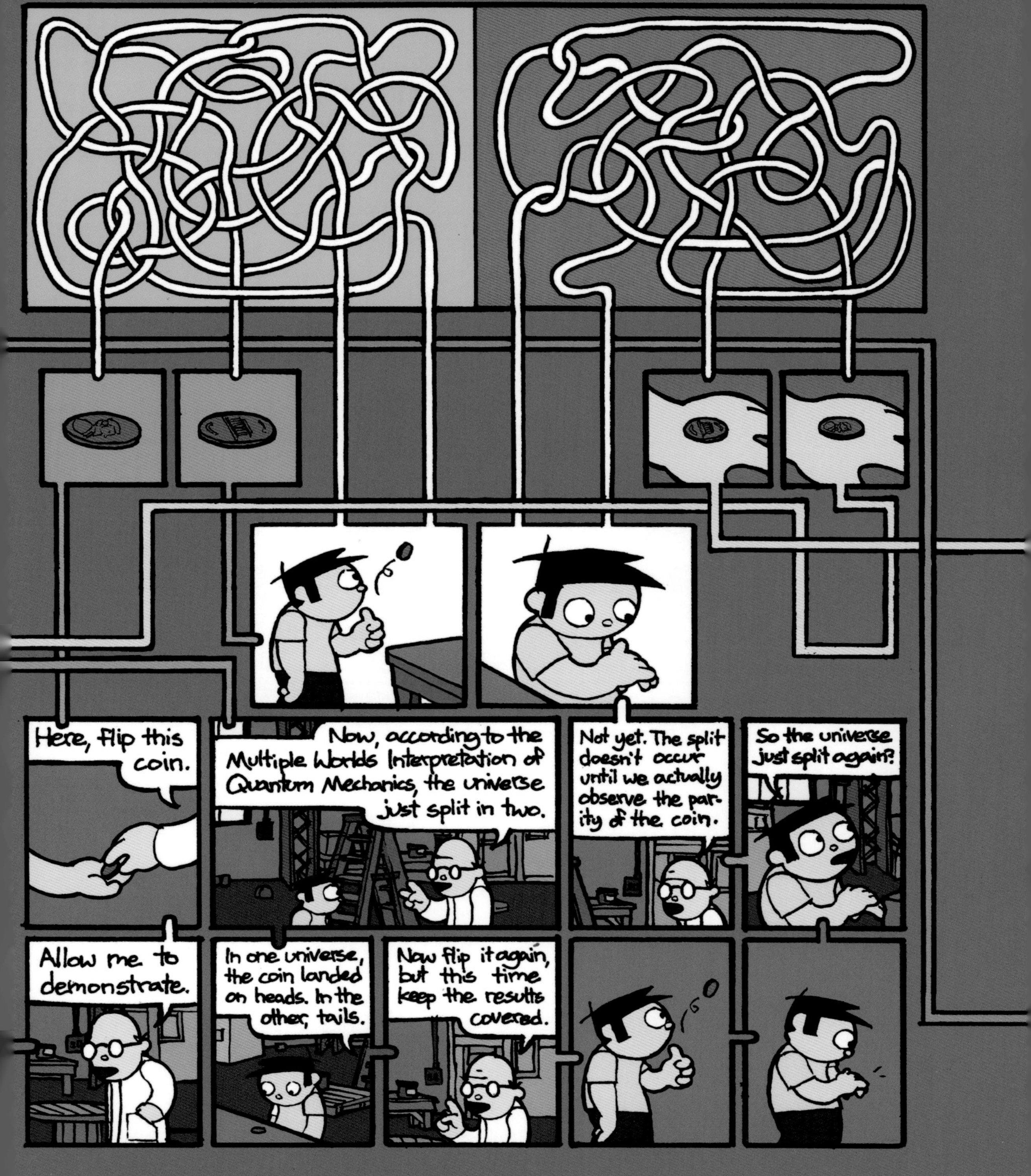

Here, flip this coin.
Now, according to the Multiple Worlds Interpretation of Quantum Mechanics, the universe just split in two.
Not yet. The split doesn't occur until we actually observe the parity of the coin.
So the universe just split again?
Allow me to demonstrate.
In one universe, the coin landed on heads. In the other, tails.
Now flip it again, but this time keep the results covered.

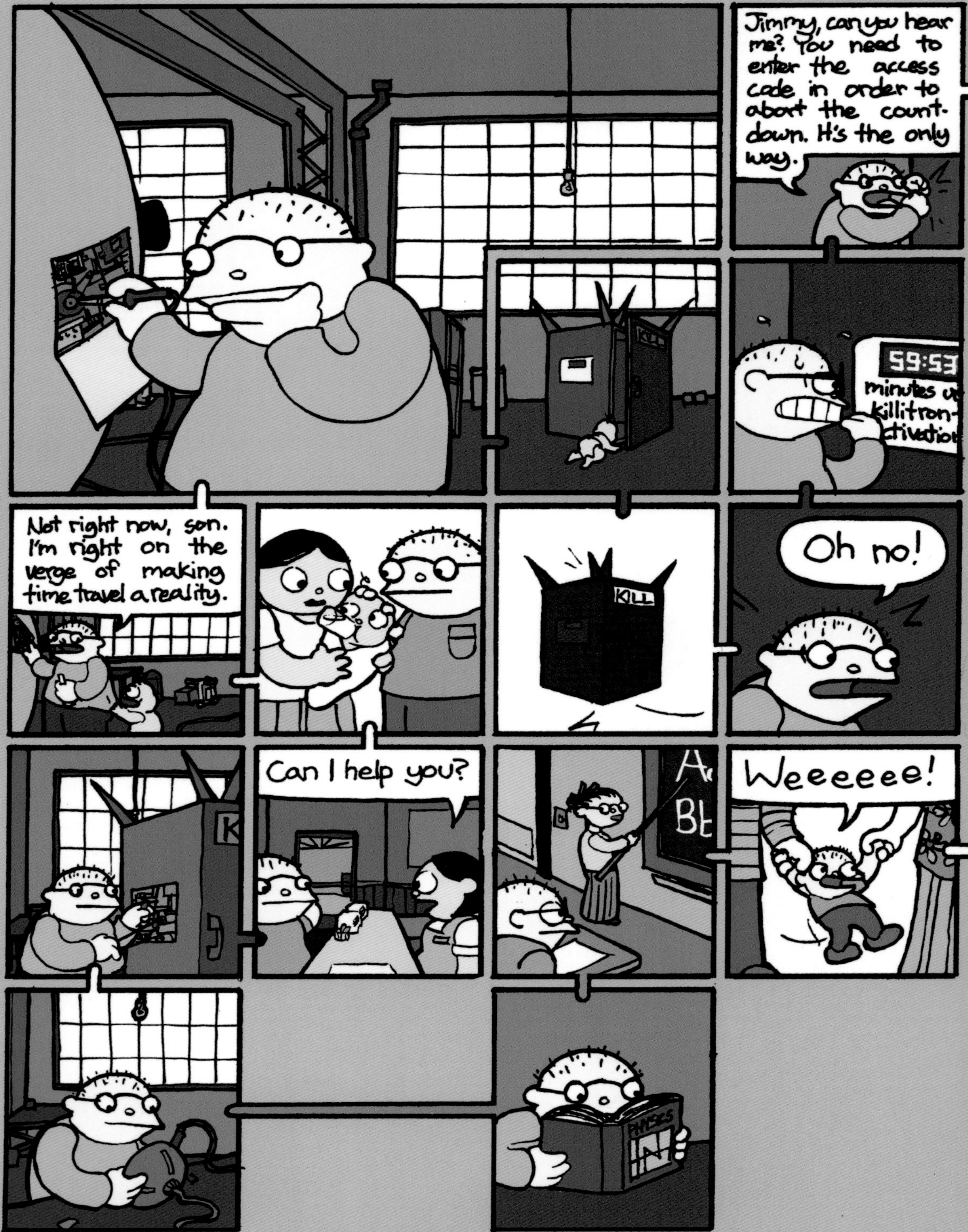

Jimmy, can you hear me? You need to enter the access code in order to abort the count-down. It's the only way.
59:53
minutes u
killitron-
ctivatio
KILL
Not right now, son. I'm right on the verge of making time travel a reality.
KILL
Oh no!
Can I help you?
Weeeeee!
PHYSICS

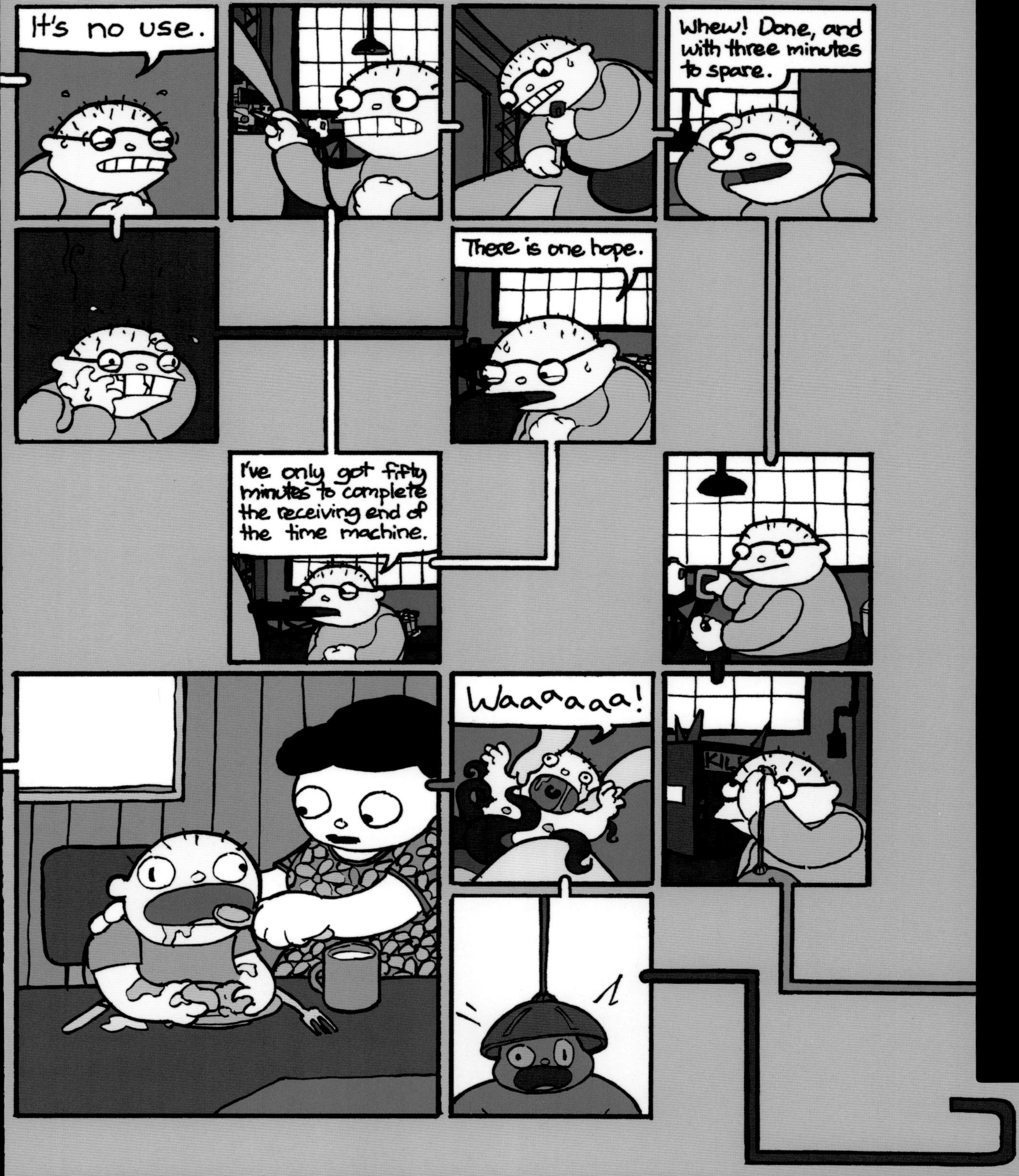
It's no use.
Whew! Done, and with three minutes to spare.
There is one hope.
I've only got fifty minutes to complete the receiving end of the time machine.
Waaaaaa!

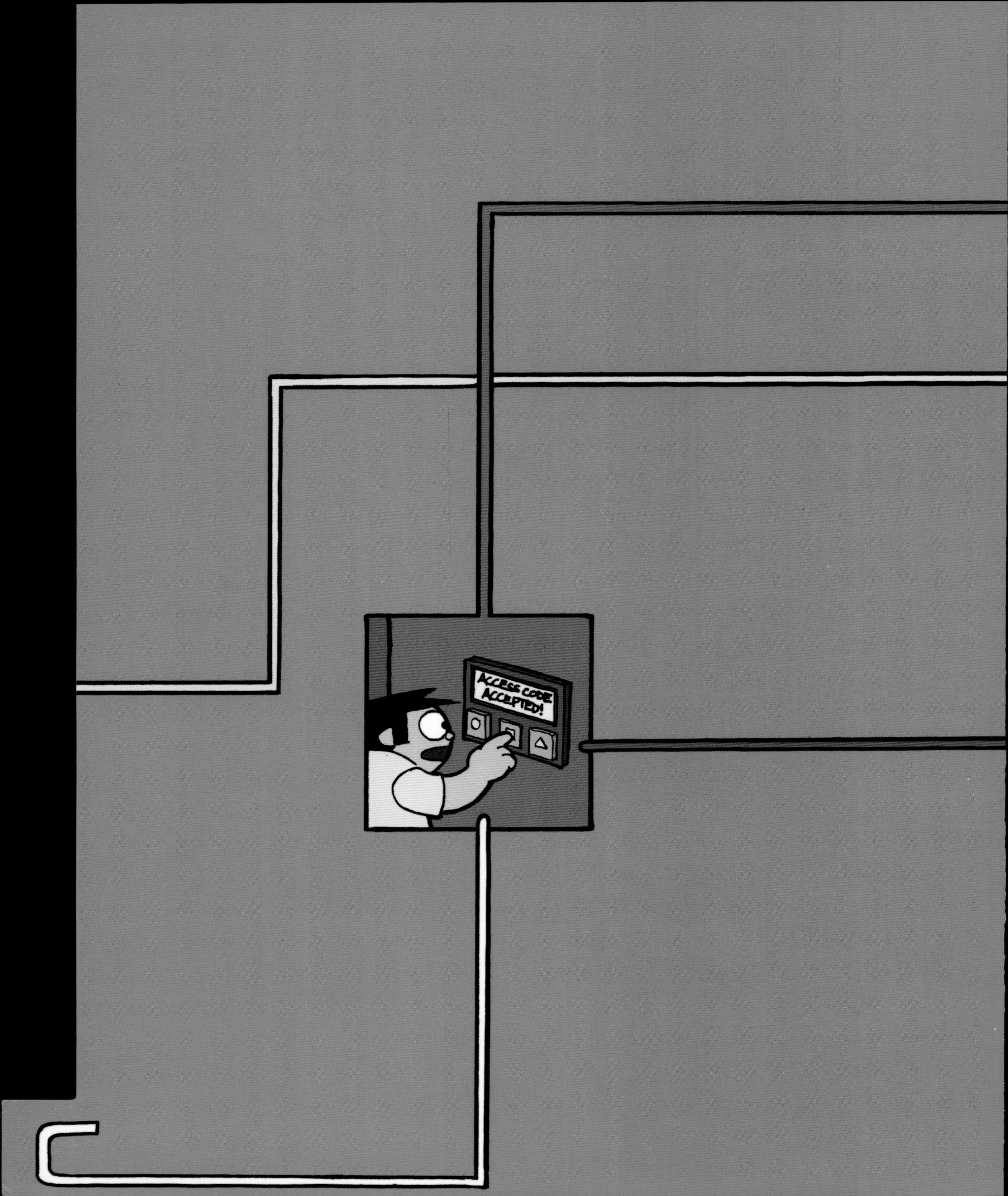
ACCESS CODE ACCEPTED!

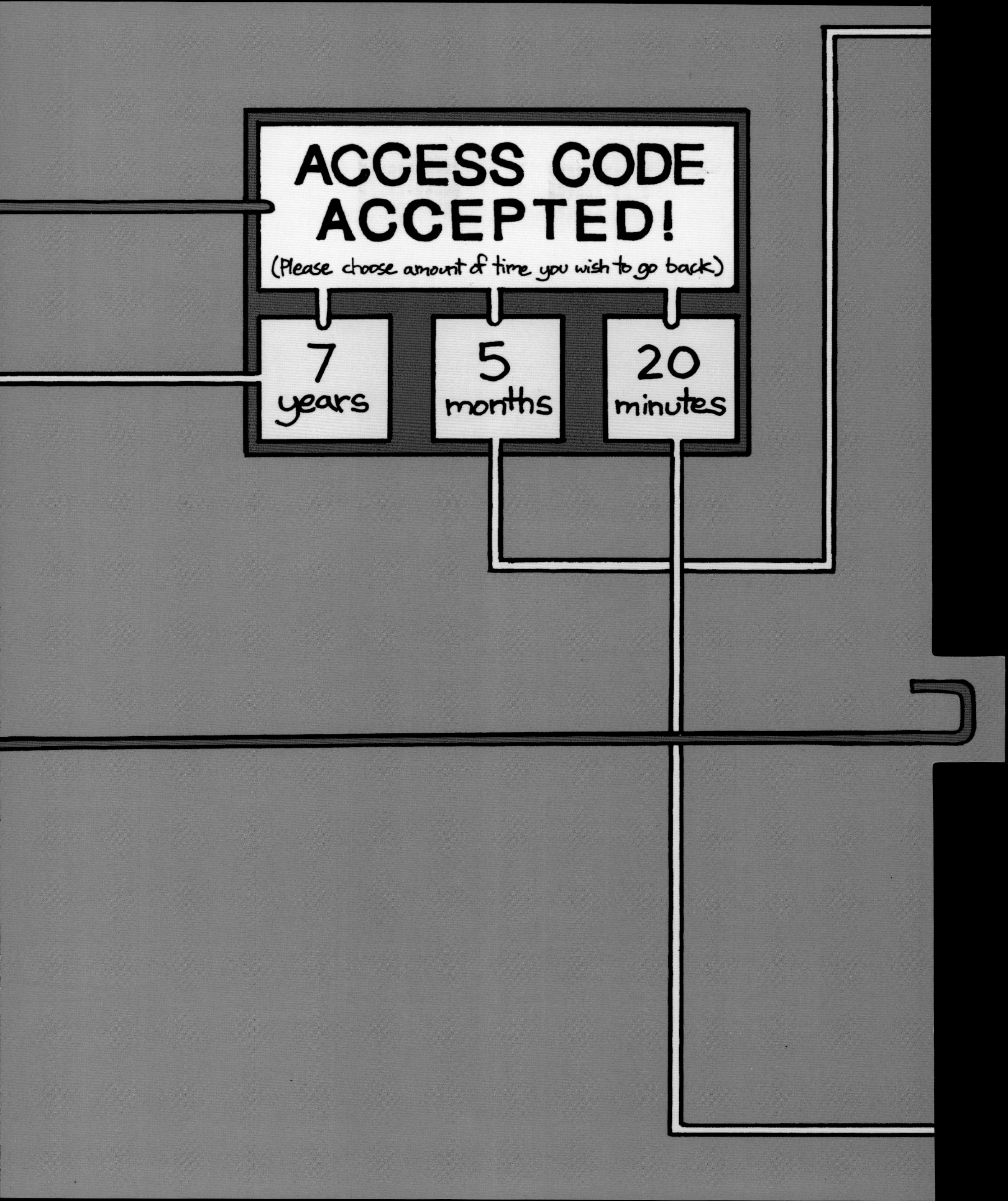
ACCESS CODE ACCEPTED!
(Please choose amount of time you wish to go back)
7 years
5 months
20 minutes

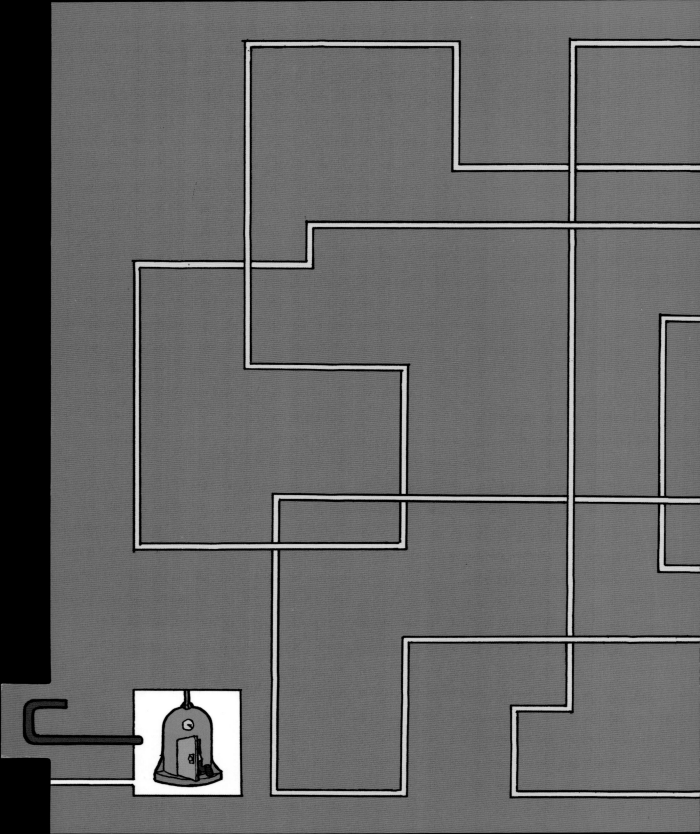

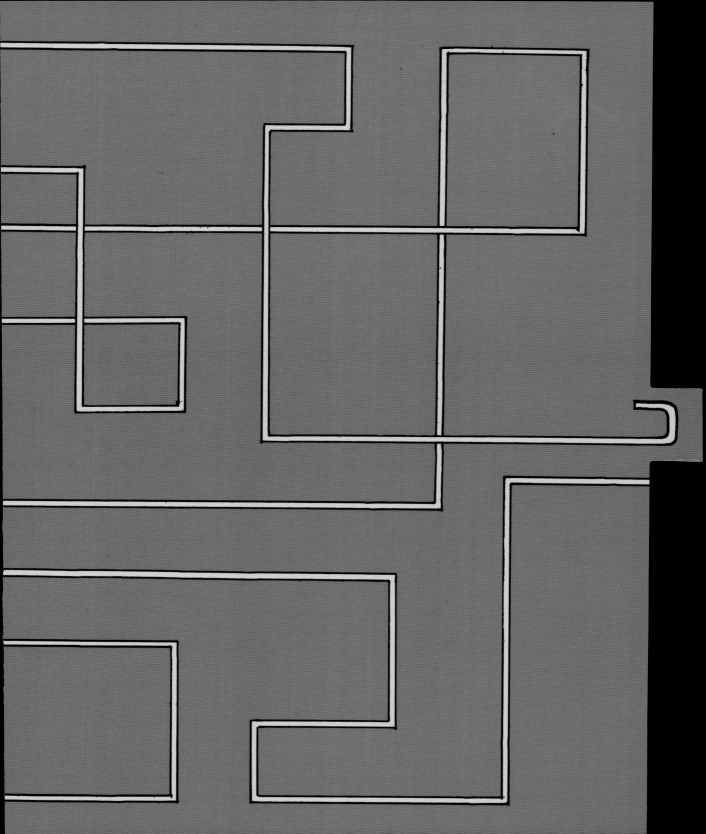

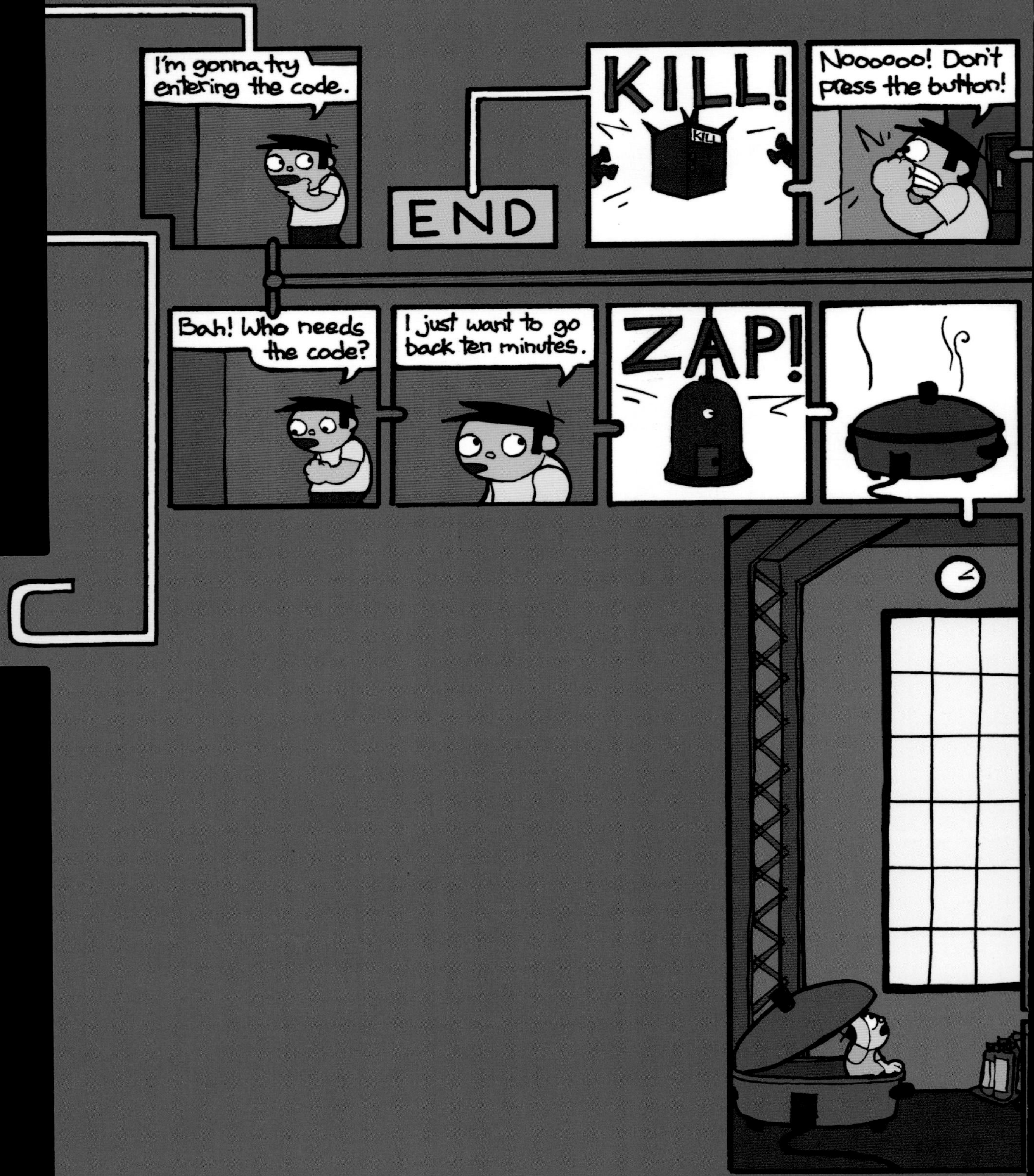
I'm gonna try entering the code.
END
KILL!
KILL
Noooooo! Don't press the button!
Bah! Who needs the code?
I just want to go back ten minutes.
ZAP!

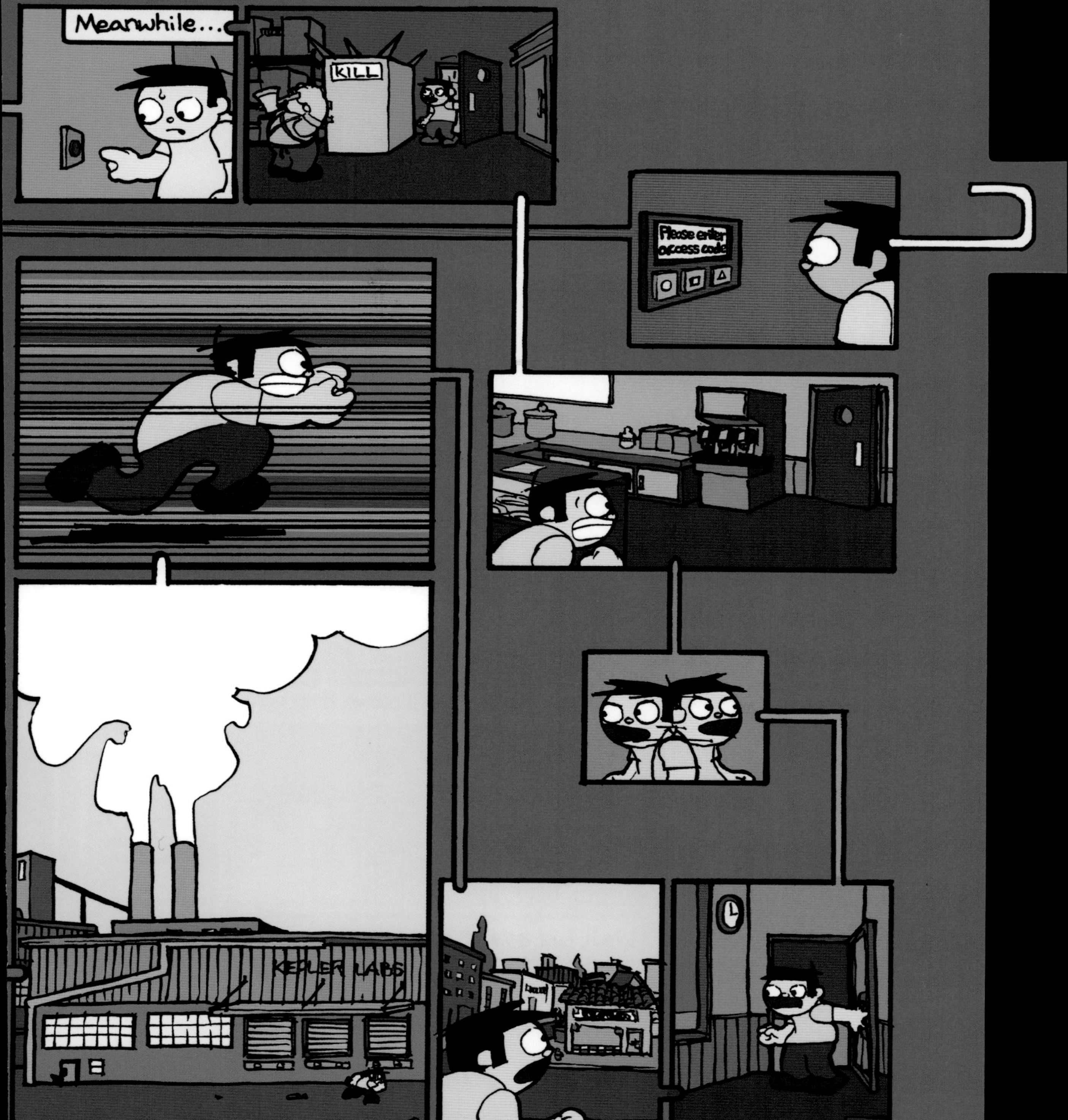
Meanwhile...
KILL
Please enter access code
KEPLER LABS

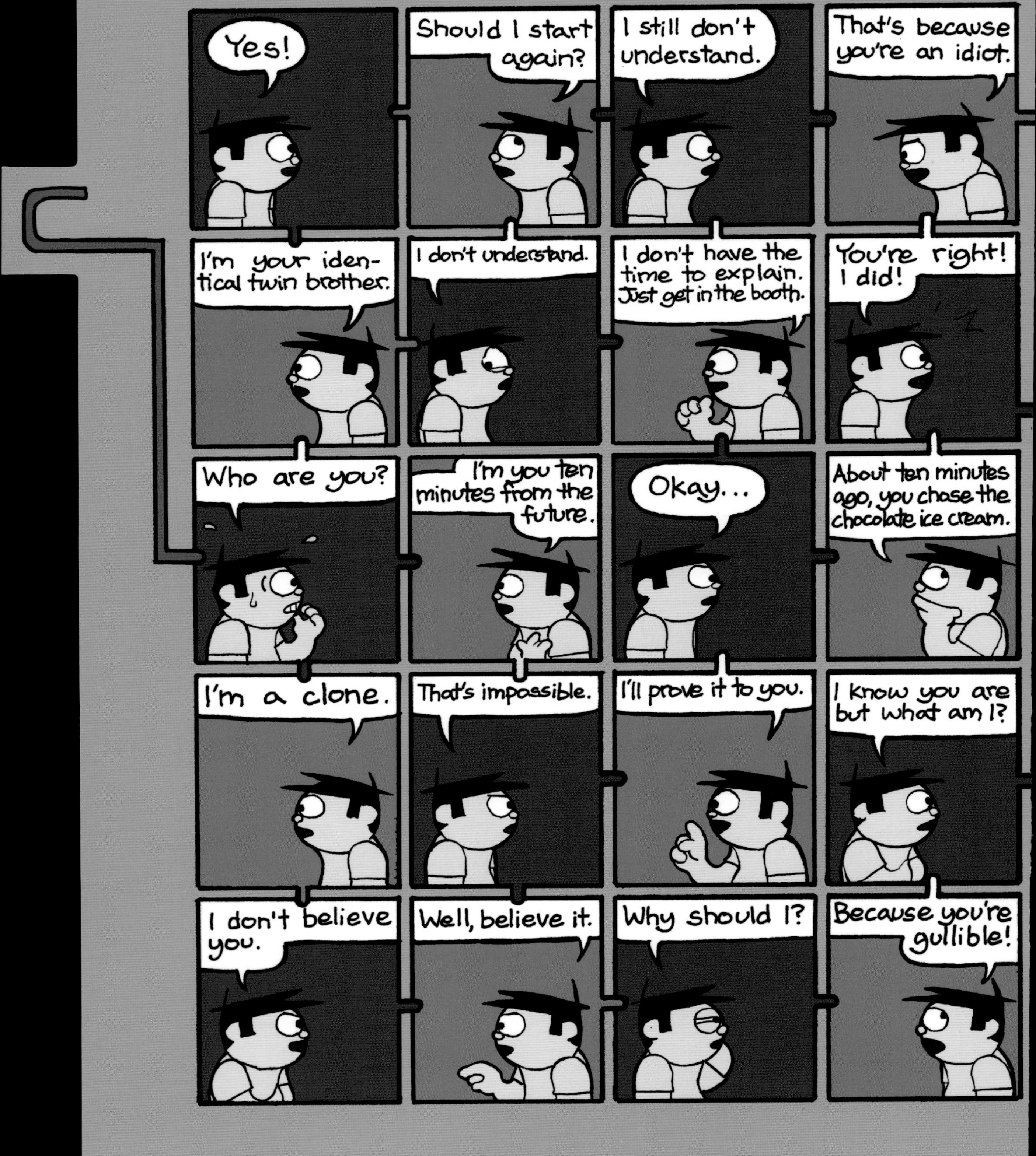
Yes!
Should I start again?
I still don't understand.
That's because you're an idiot.
I'm your identical twin brother.
I don't understand.
I don't have the time to explain. Just get in the booth.
You're right! I did!
Who are you?
I'm you ten minutes from the future.
Okay...
About ten minutes ago, you chose the chocolate ice cream.
I'm a clone.
That's impossible.
I'll prove it to you.
I know you are but what am I?
I don't believe you.
Well, believe it.
Why should I?
Because you're gullible!

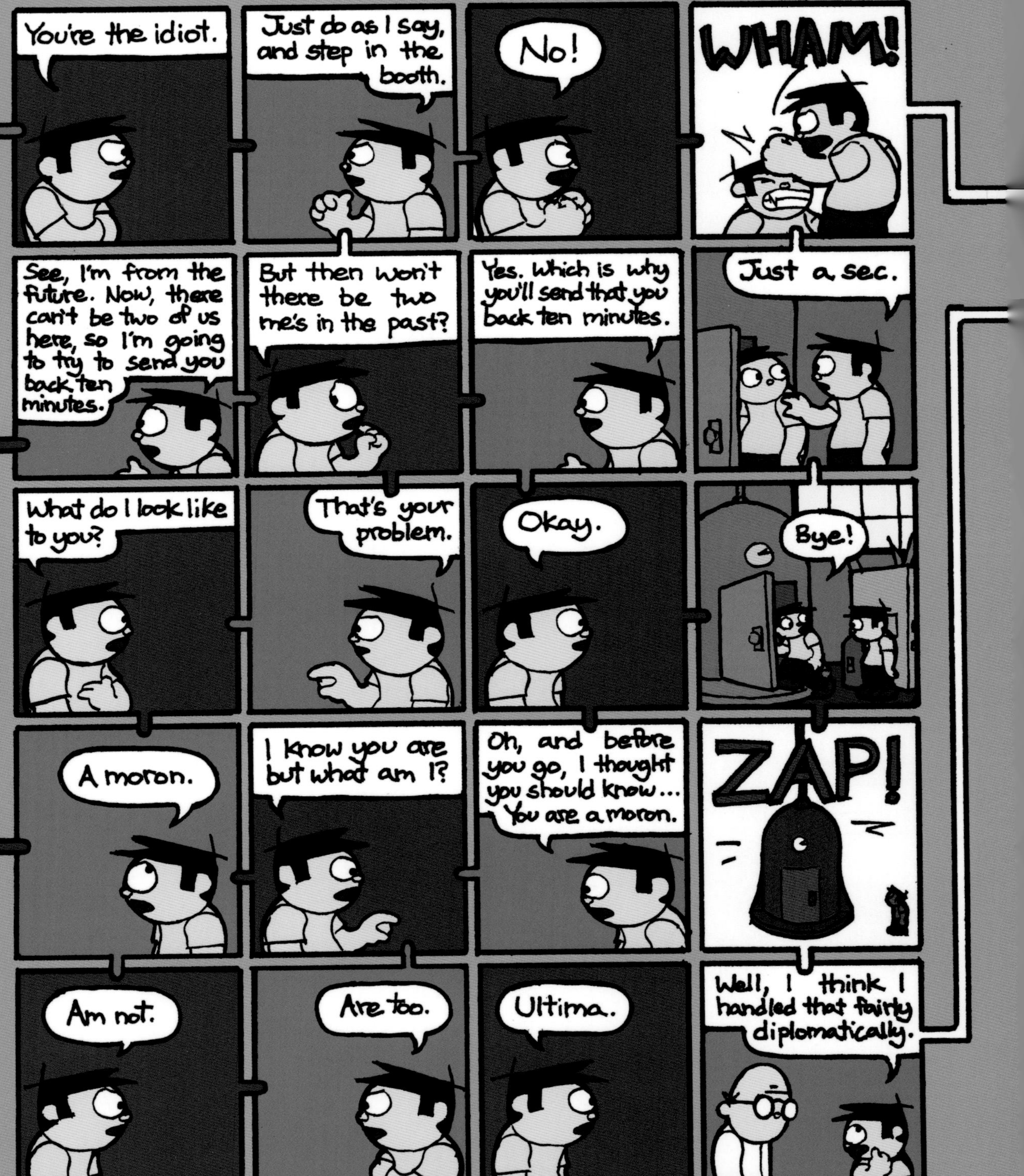
You're the idiot.
Just do as I say, and step in the booth.
No!
WHAM!
See, I'm from the future. Now, there can't be two of us here, so I'm going to try to send you back ten minutes.
But then won't there be two me's in the past?
Yes. Which is why you'll send that you back ten minutes.
Just a sec.
What do I look like to you?
That's your problem.
Okay.
Bye!
A moron.
I know you are but what am I?
Oh, and before you go, I thought you should know... You are a moron.
ZAP!
Am not.
Are too.
Ultima.
Well, I think I handled that fairly diplomatically.

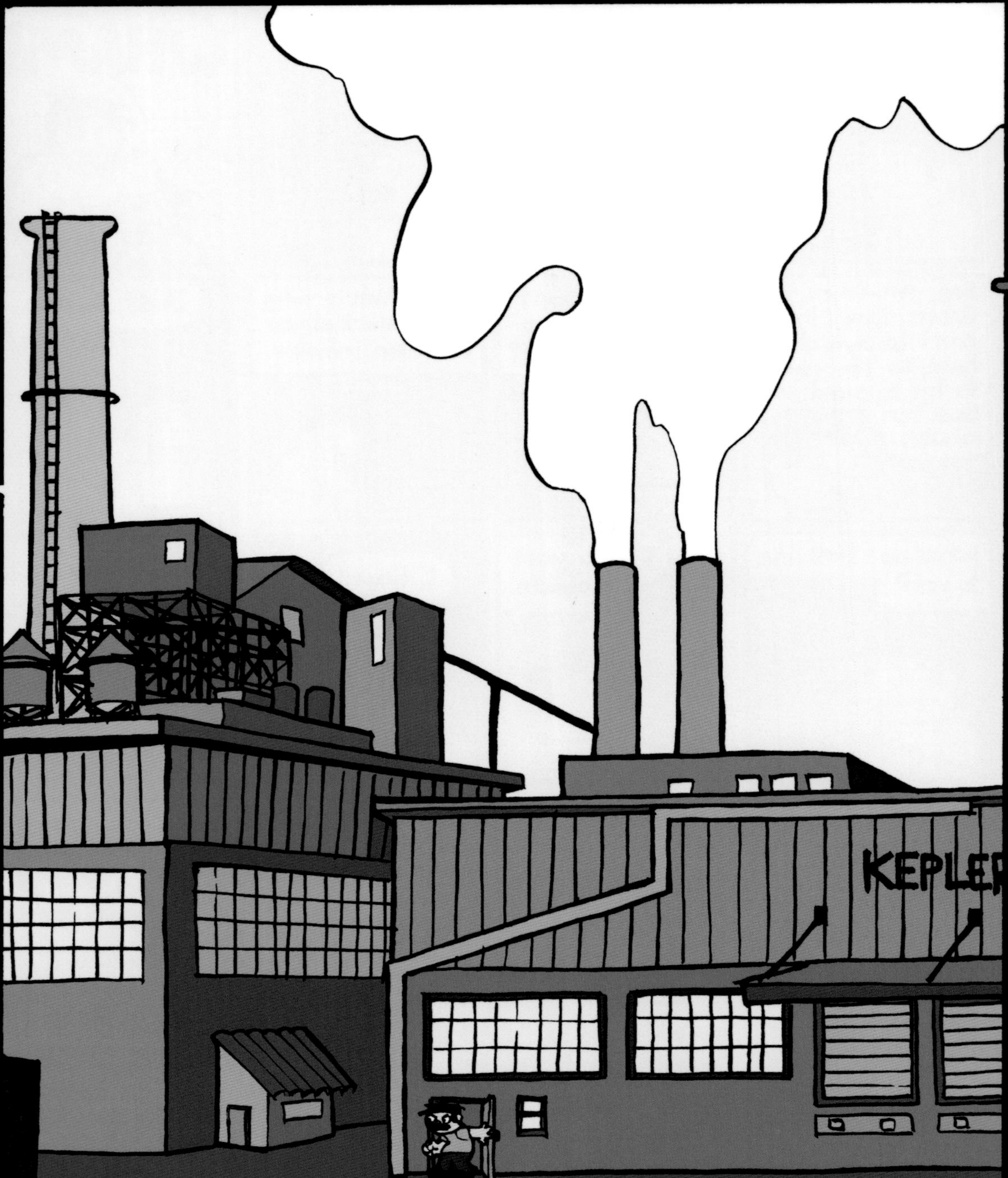
KEPLER

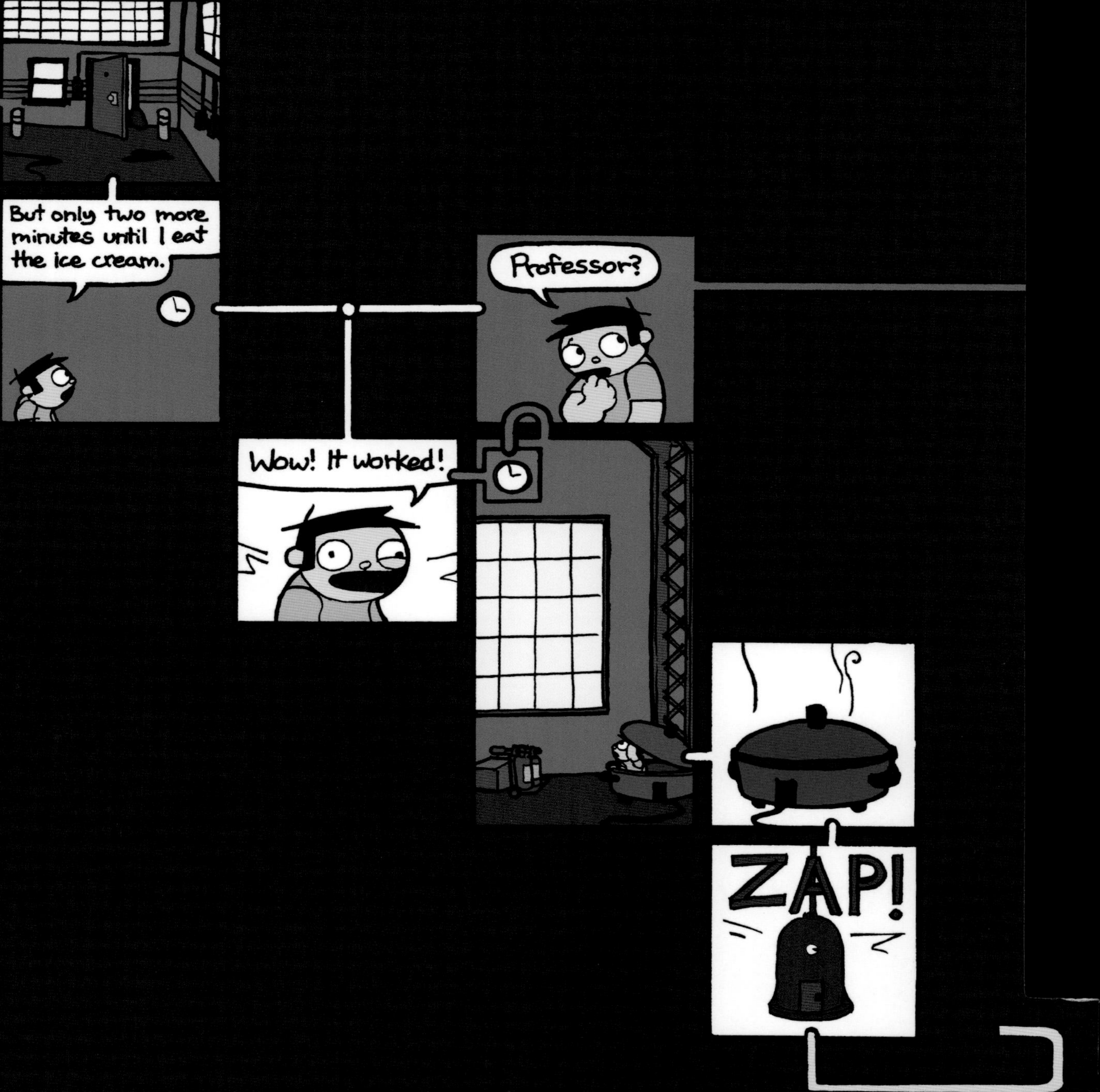
But only two more minutes until I eat the ice cream.
Professor?
Wow! It worked!
ZAP!

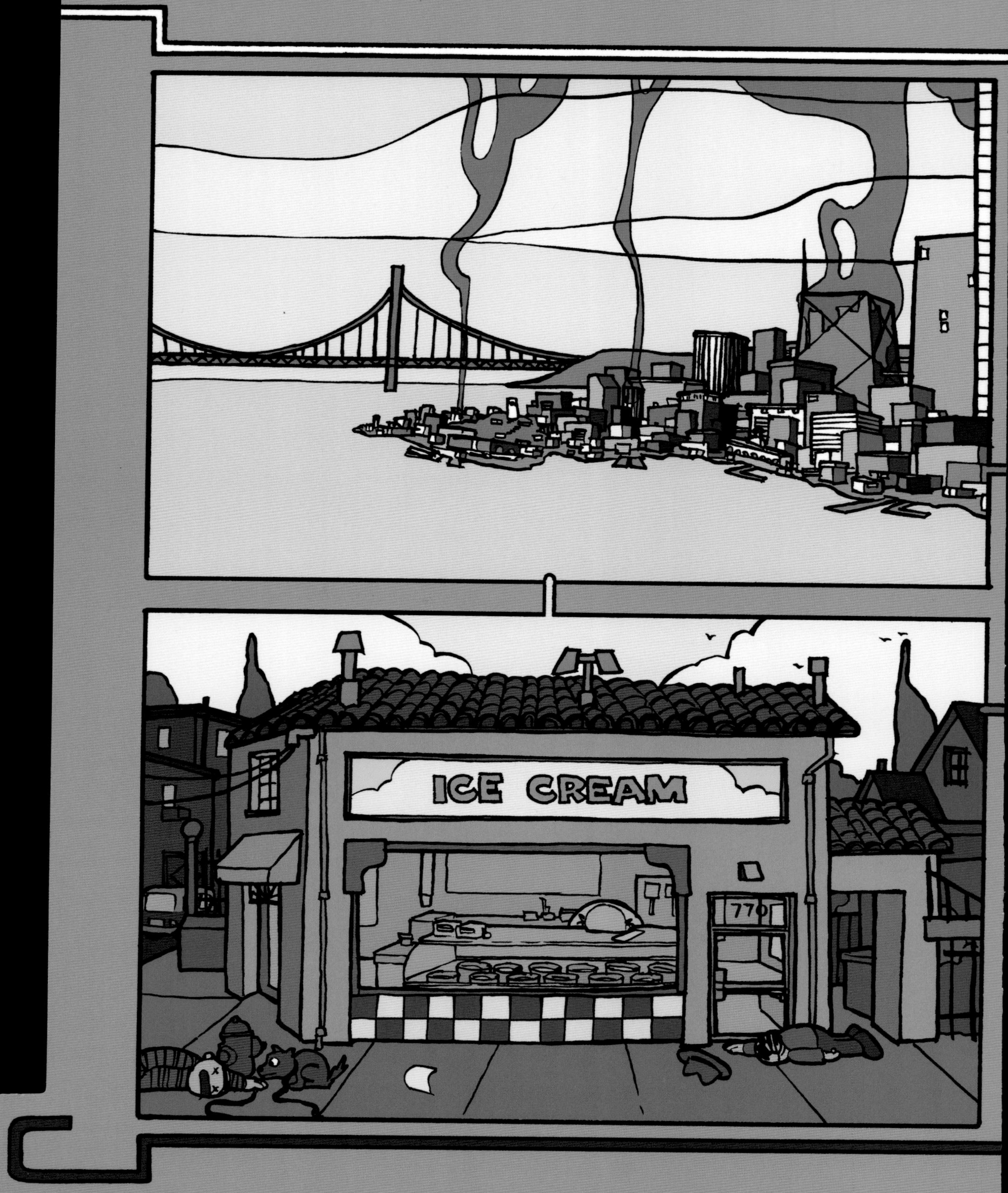
ICE CREAM
770

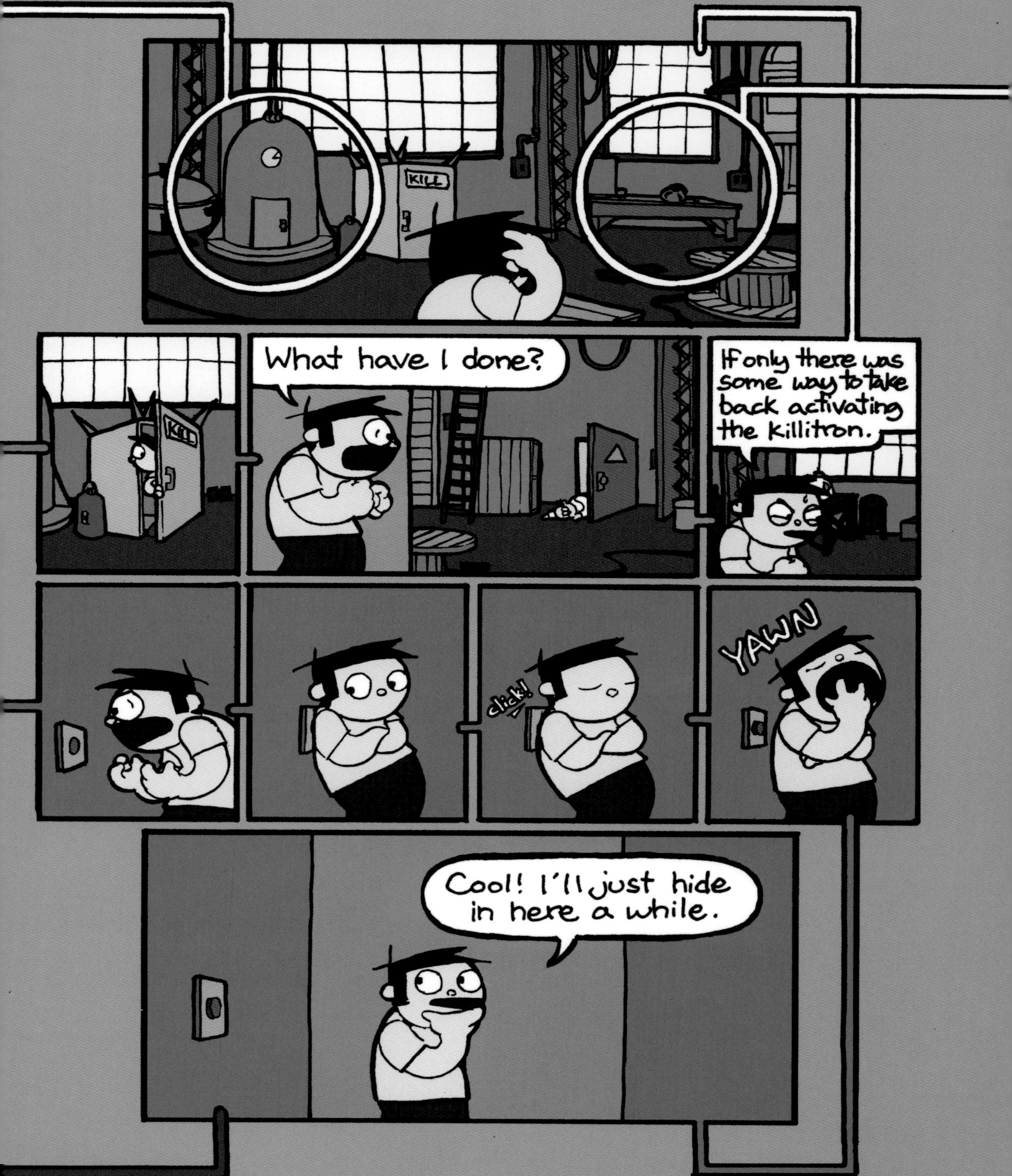
KILL
KILL
What have I done?
If only there was some way to take back activating the killitron.
click!
YAWN
Cool! I'll just hide in here a while.

SQUID

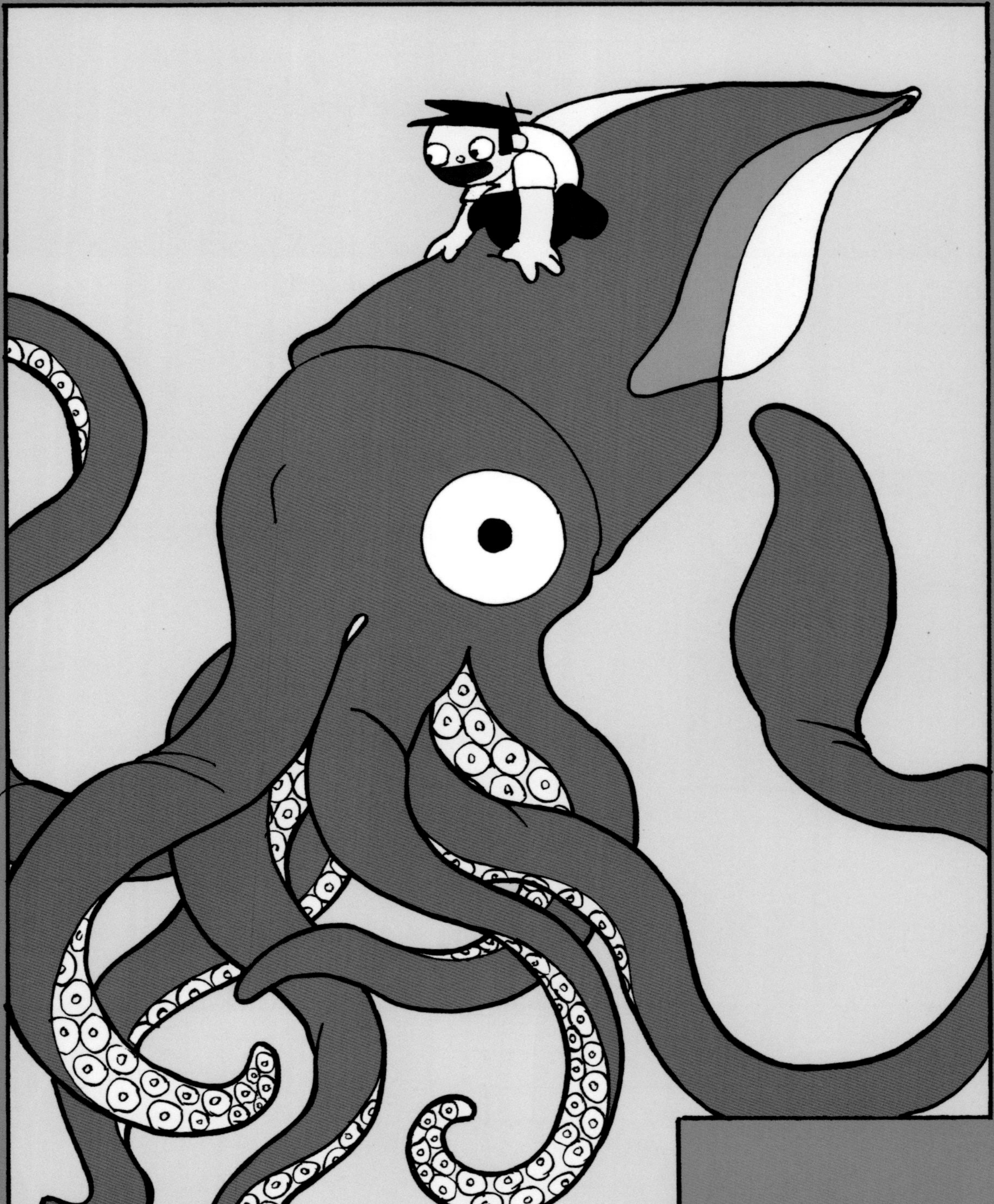

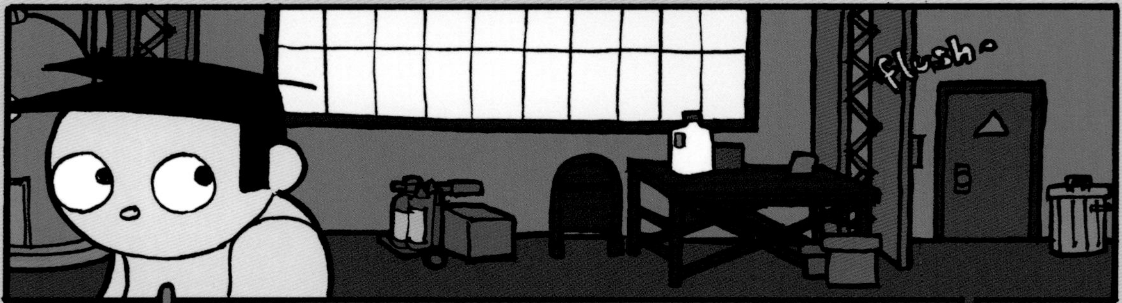
flush.

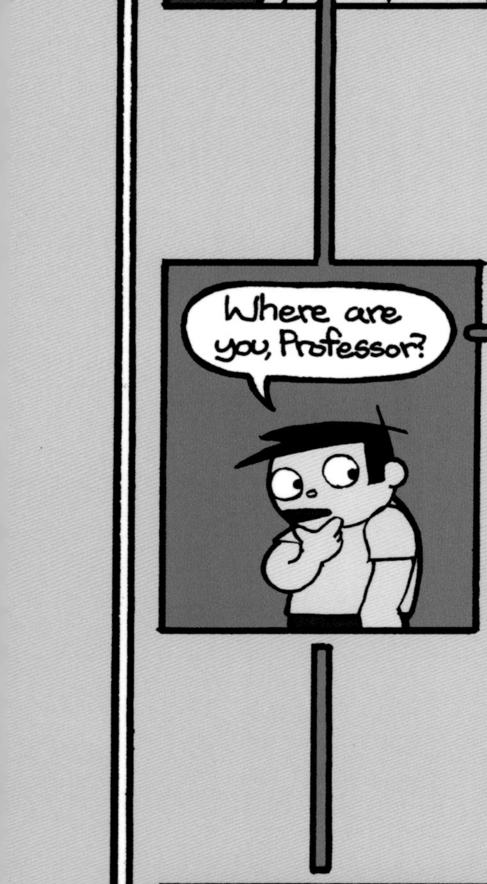
Where are you, Professor?

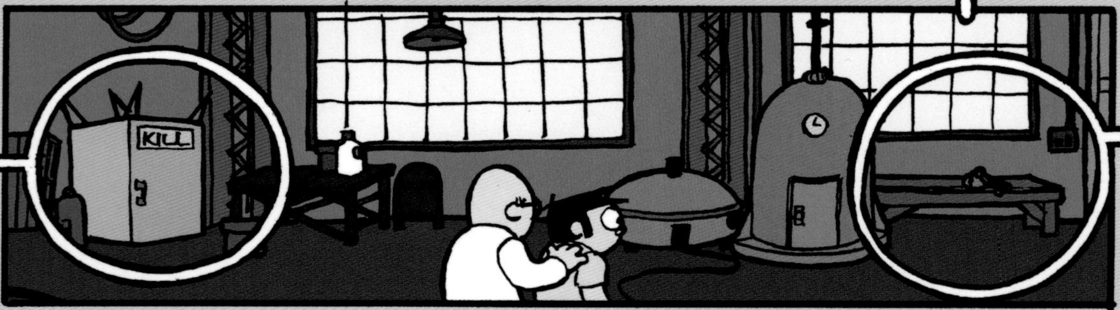
KILL

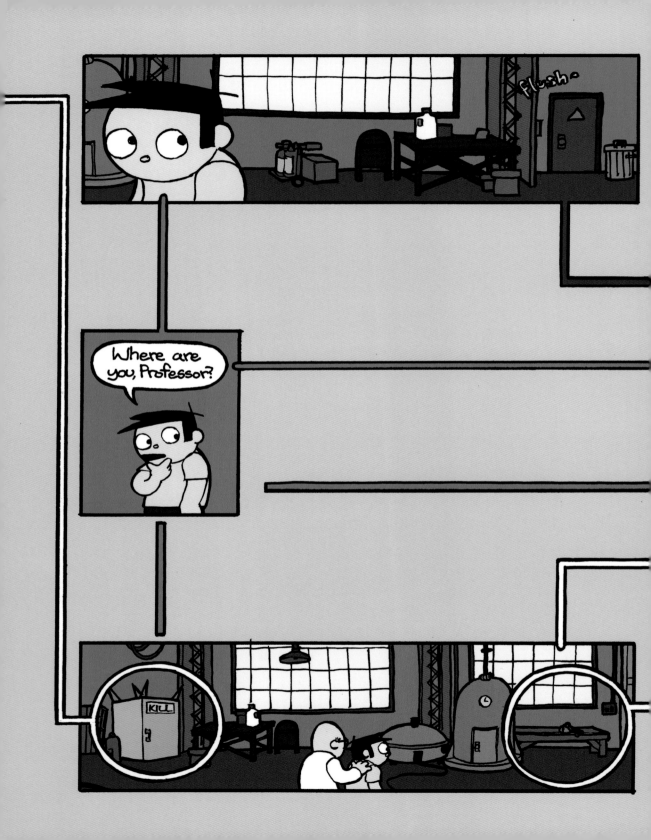

Why, hello there.
Hi. I'm Jimmy!
Welcome to my lab, Jimmy.
Would you like to play with some of my inventions?
Okay.
Well, my time machine is warming up right now.
But you're wel-come to play with the Killitron or the SQUID.
KILL
KILL

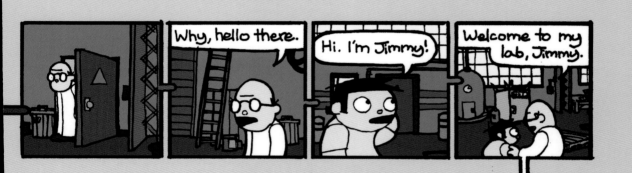

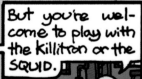

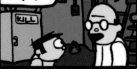

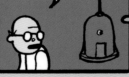

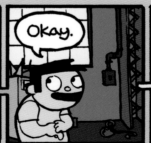

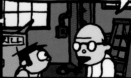

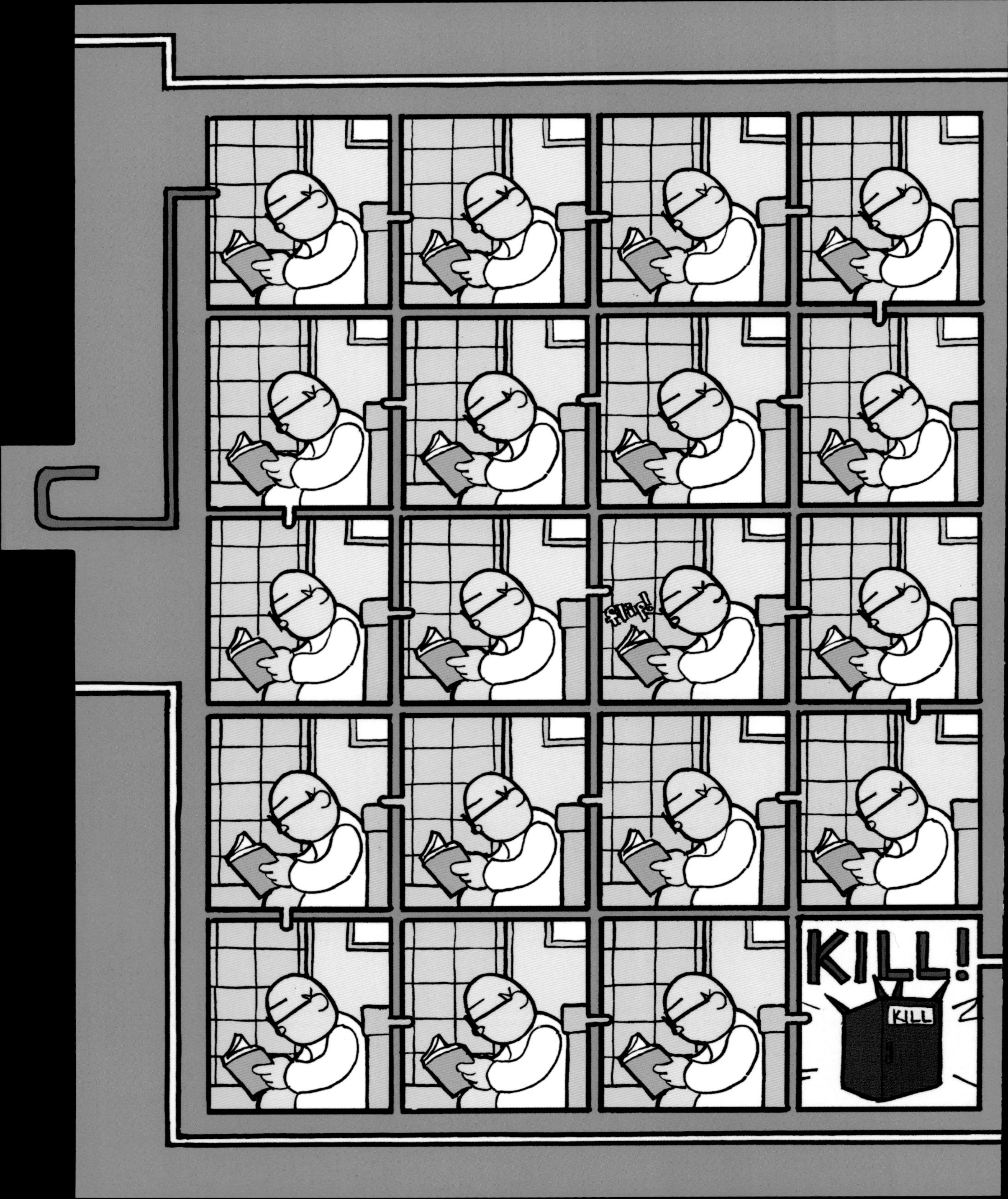
flip!
KILL!
KILL

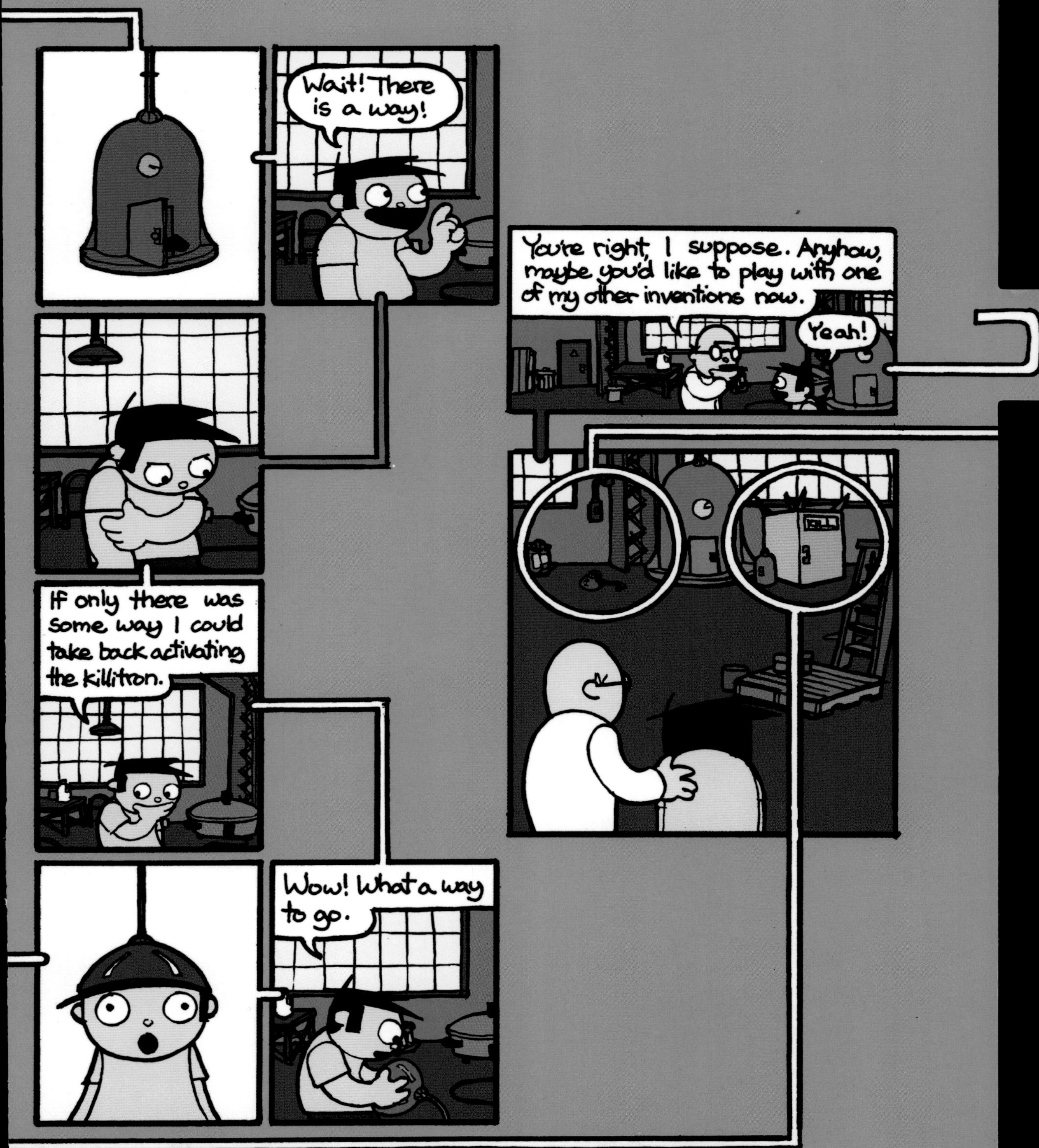
Wait! There is a way!
If only there was some way I could take back activating the killitron.
Wow! What a way to go.
You're right, I suppose. Anyhow, maybe you'd like to play with one of my other inventions now.
Yeah!

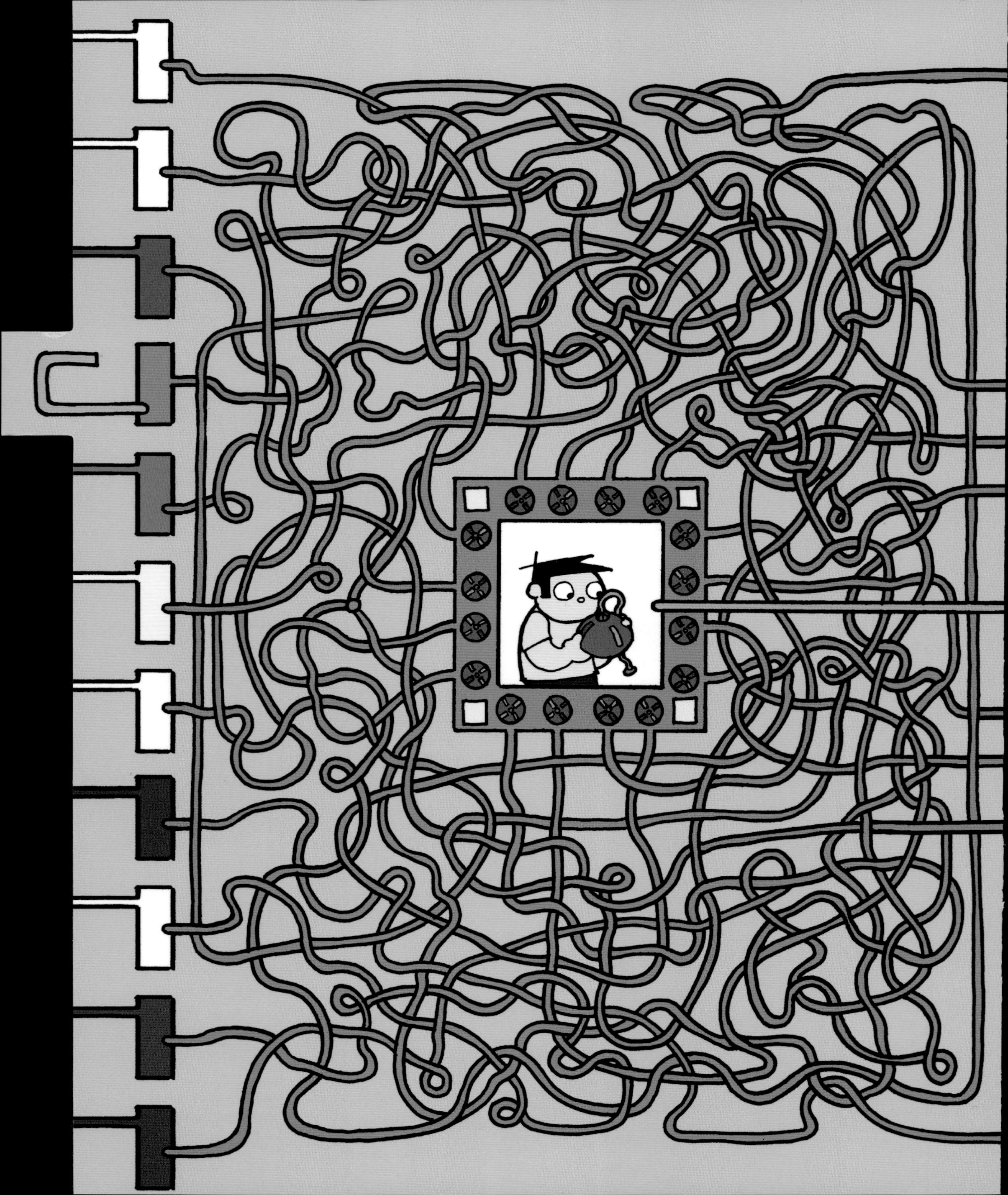

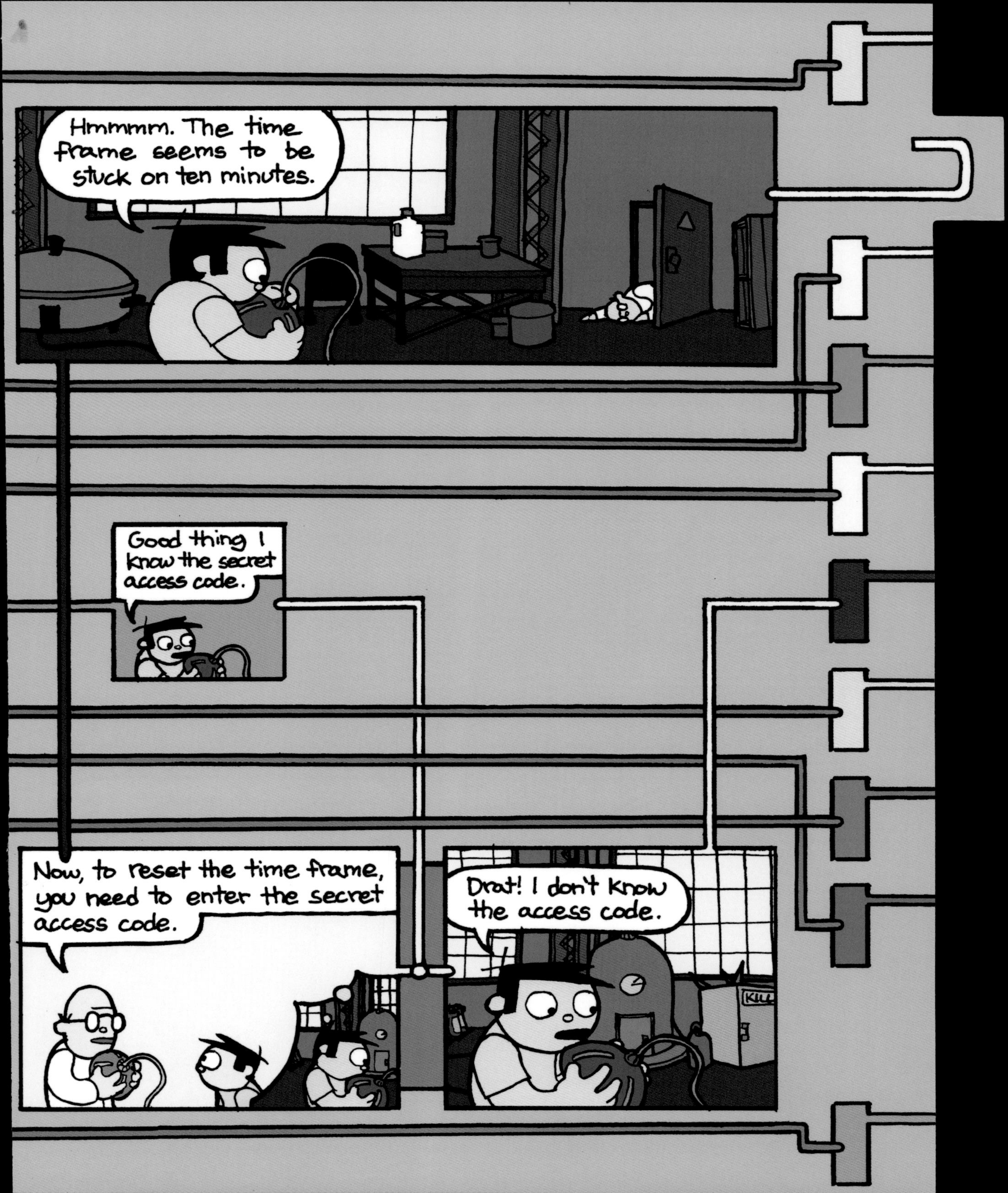
Hmmmm. The time frame seems to be stuck on ten minutes.
Good thing I know the secret access code.
Now, to reset the time frame, you need to enter the secret access code.
Drat! I don't know the access code.

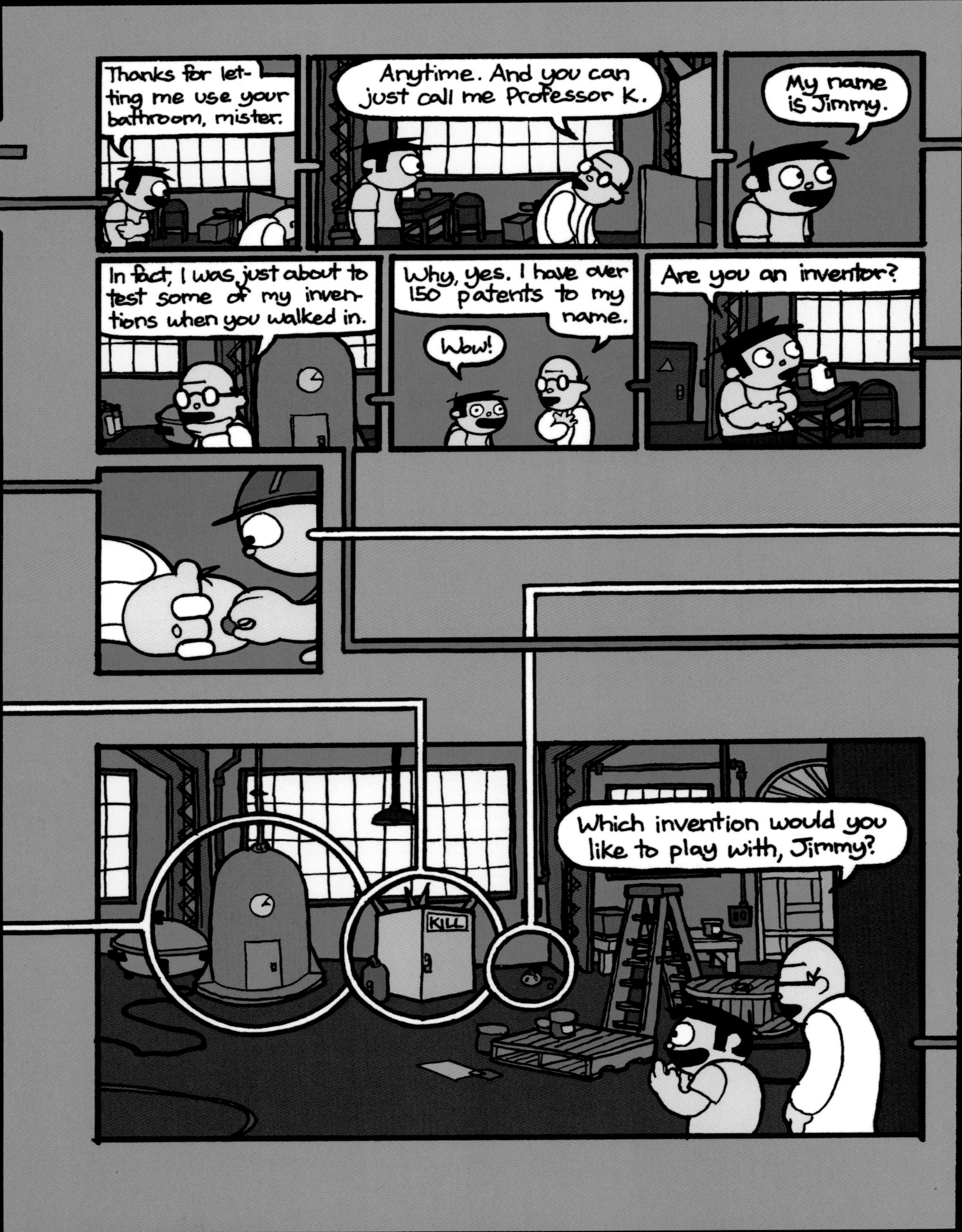
Thanks for letting me use your bathroom, mister.
Anytime. And you can just call me Professor K.
My name is Jimmy.
In fact, I was just about to test some of my inventions when you walked in.
Why, yes. I have over 150 patents to my name.
Wow!
Are you an inventor?
KILL
Which invention would you like to play with, Jimmy?

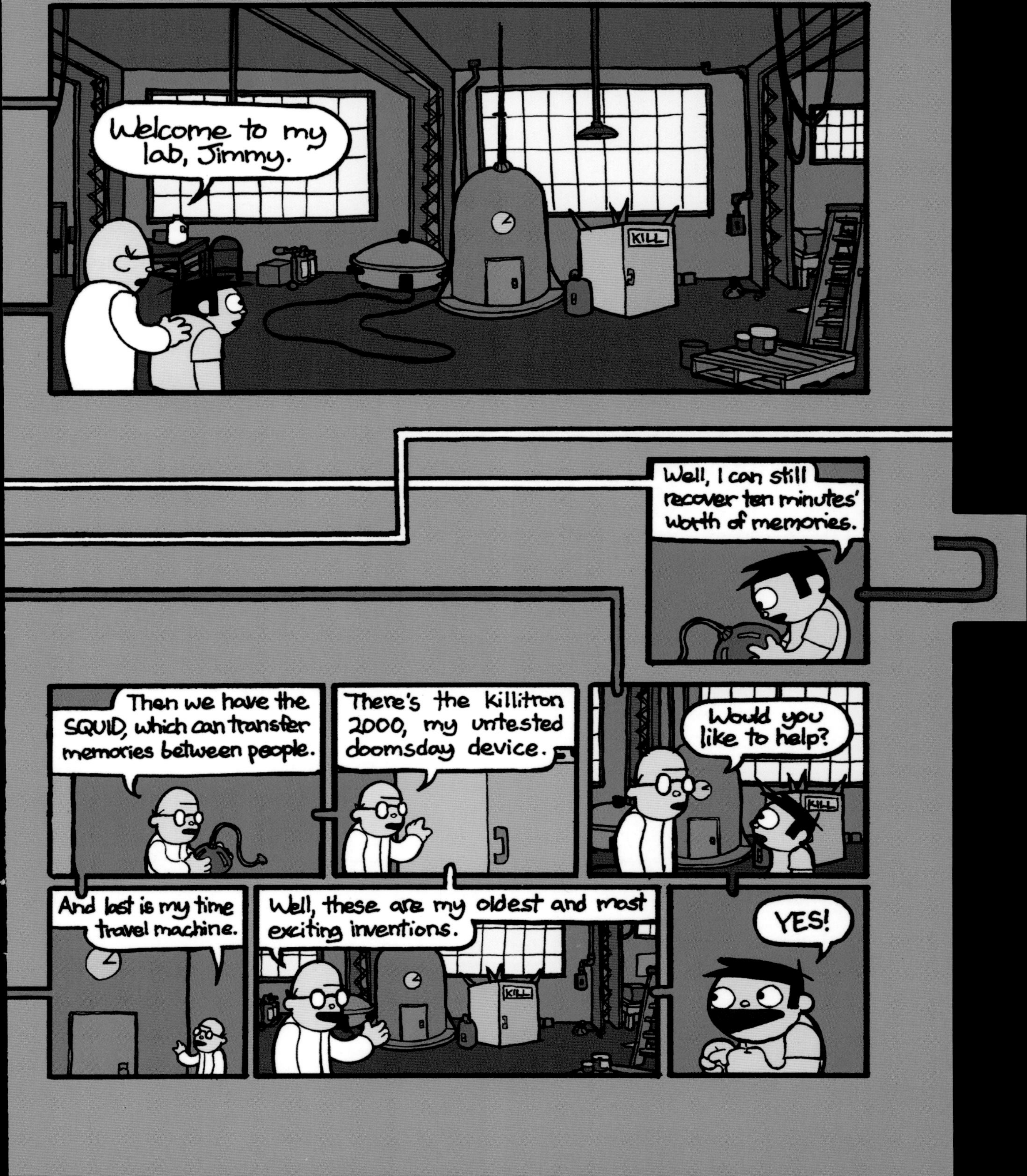
Welcome to my lab, Jimmy.
KILL
Well, I can still recover ten minutes' worth of memories.
Then we have the SQUID, which can transfer memories between people.
There's the Killitron 2000, my untested doomsday device.
Would you like to help?
And last is my time travel machine.
Well, these are my oldest and most exciting inventions.
YES!

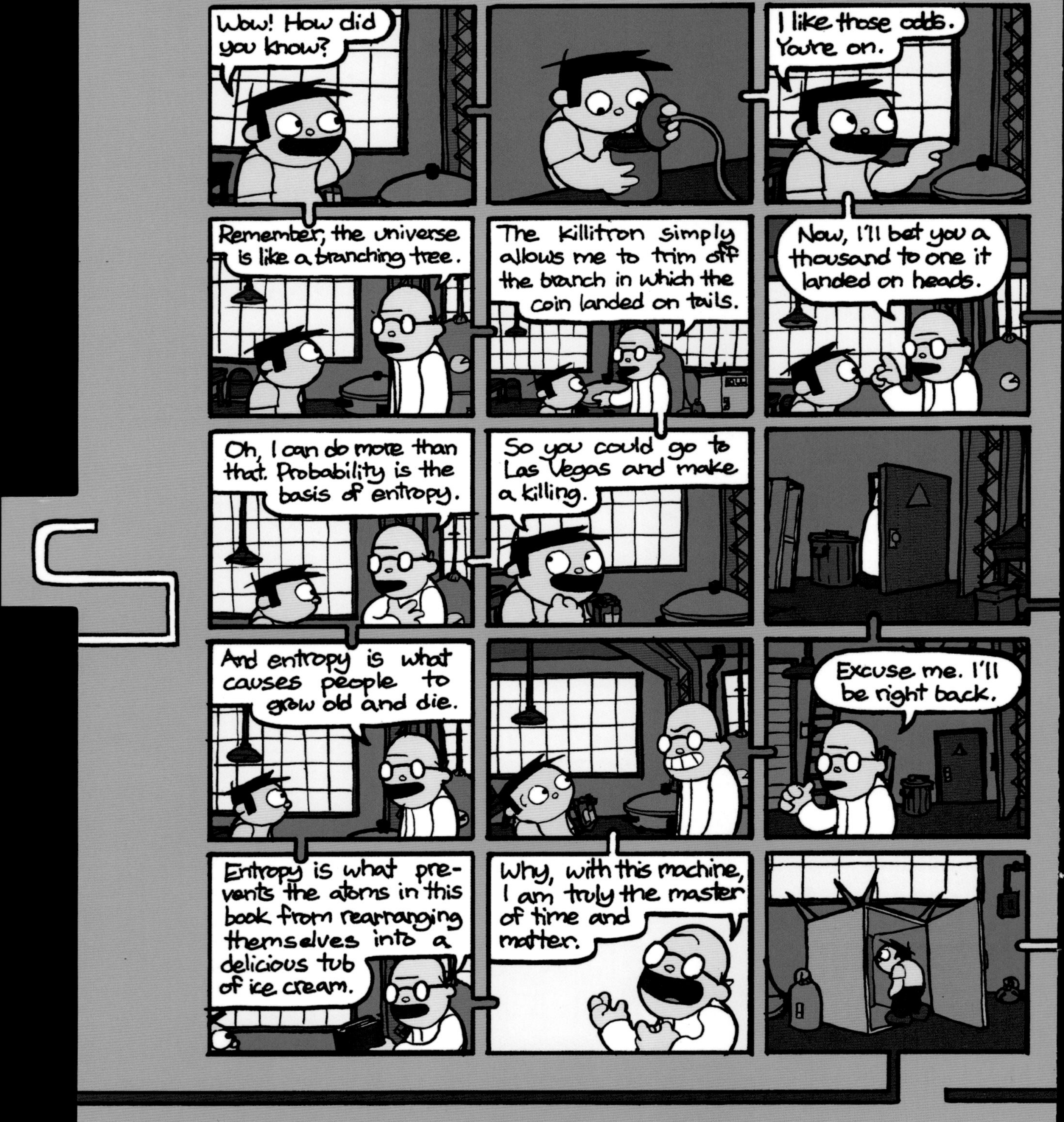

Wow! How did you know?
I like those odds. You're on.
Remember, the universe is like a branching tree.
The killitron simply allows me to trim off the branch in which the coin landed on tails.
Now, I'll bet you a thousand to one it landed on heads.
Oh, I can do more than that. Probability is the basis of entropy.
So you could go to Las Vegas and make a killing.
And entropy is what causes people to grow old and die.
Excuse me. I'll be right back.
Entropy is what prevents the atoms in this book from rearranging themselves into a delicious tub of ice cream.
Why, with this machine, I am truly the master of time and matter.

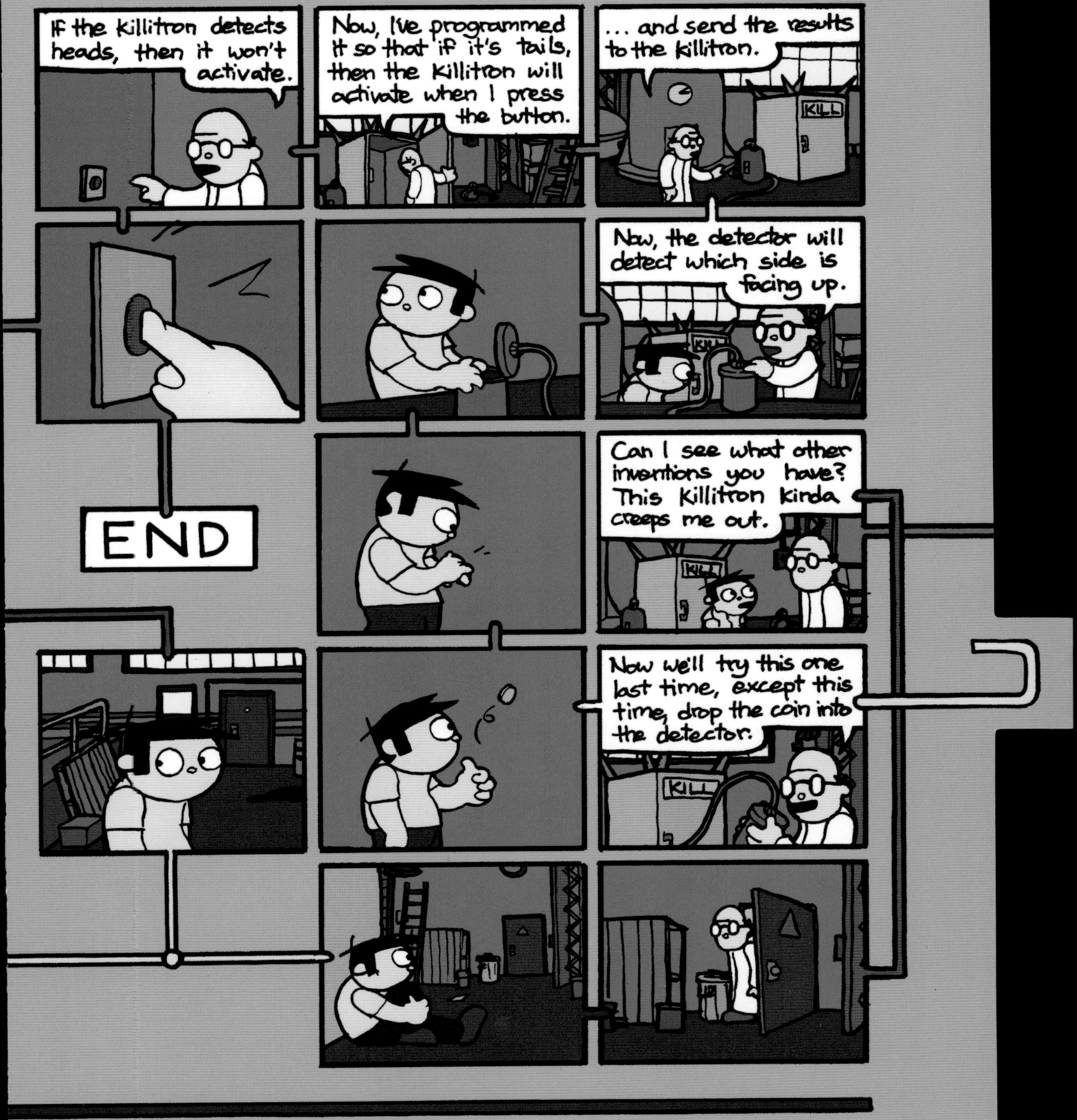
If the killitron detects heads, then it won't activate.
Now, I've programmed it so that if it's tails, then the Killitron will activate when I press the button.
... and send the results to the killitron.
KILL
Now, the detector will detect which side is facing up.
END
Can I see what other inventions you have? This Killitron kinda creeps me out.
Now we'll try this one last time, except this time, drop the coin into the detector.

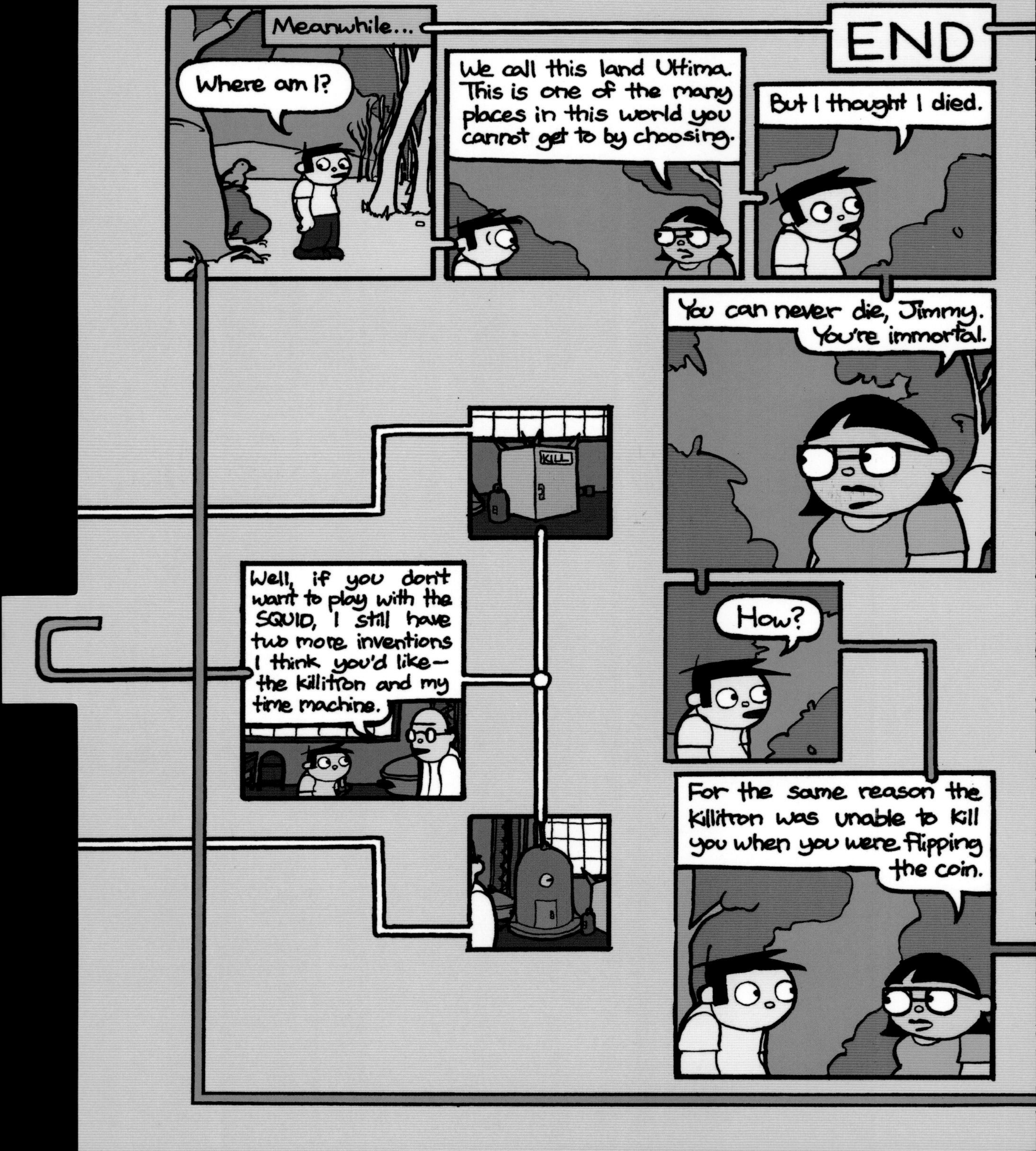
Meanwhile...
Where am I?
We call this land Ultima. This is one of the many places in this world you cannot get to by choosing.
But I thought I died.
END
KILL
Well, if you don't want to play with the SQUID, I still have two more inventions I think you'd like—the killitron and my time machine.
You can never die, Jimmy. You're immortal.
How?
For the same reason the killitron was unable to kill you when you were flipping the coin.

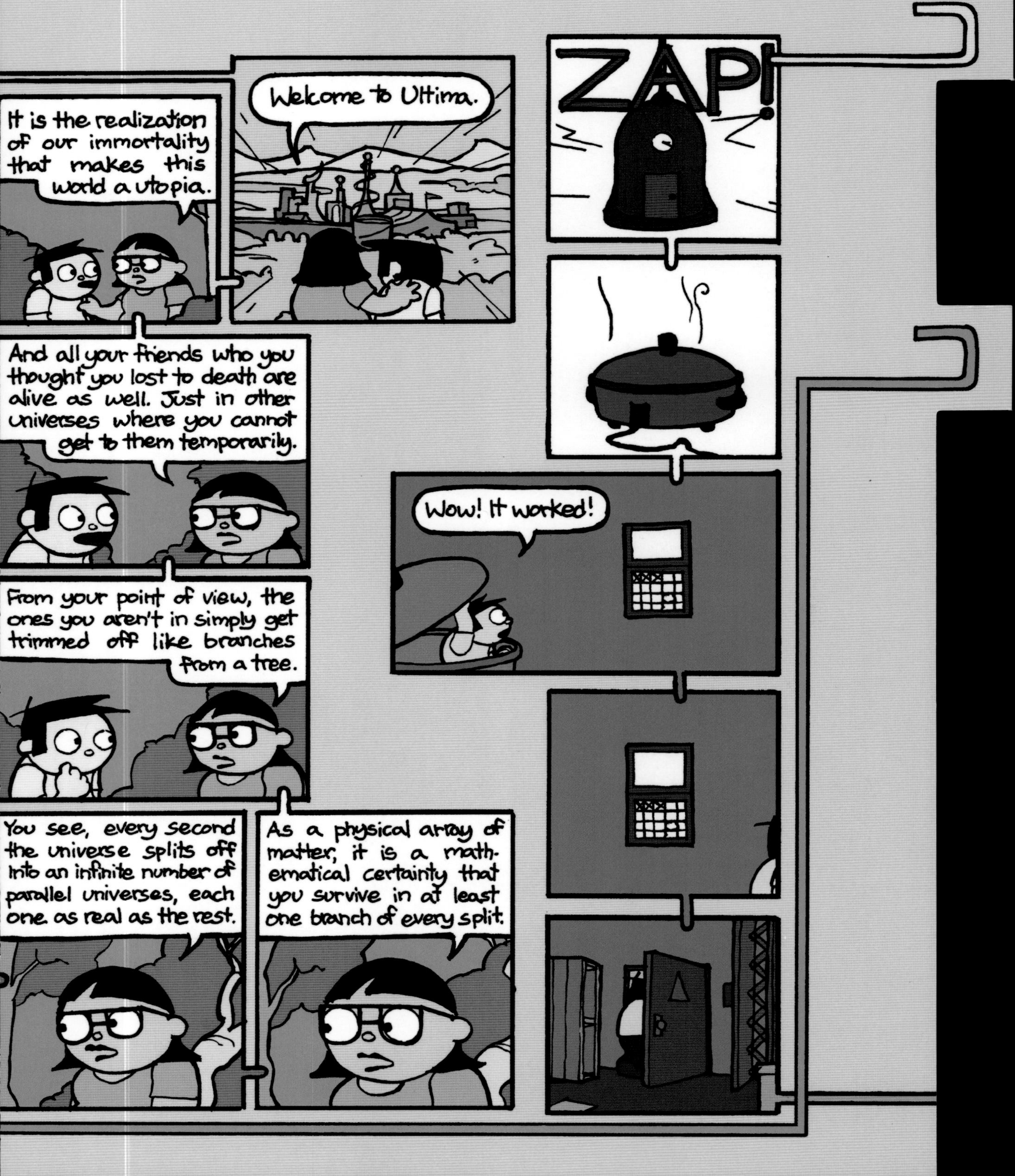
It is the realization of our immortality that makes this world a utopia.
Welcome to Ultima.
ZAP!
And all your friends who you thought you lost to death are alive as well. Just in other universes where you cannot get to them temporarily.
Wow! It worked!
From your point of view, the ones you aren't in simply get trimmed off like branches from a tree.
You see, every second the universe splits off into an infinite number of parallel universes, each one as real as the rest.
As a physical array of matter, it is a mathematical certainty that you survive in at least one branch of every split.

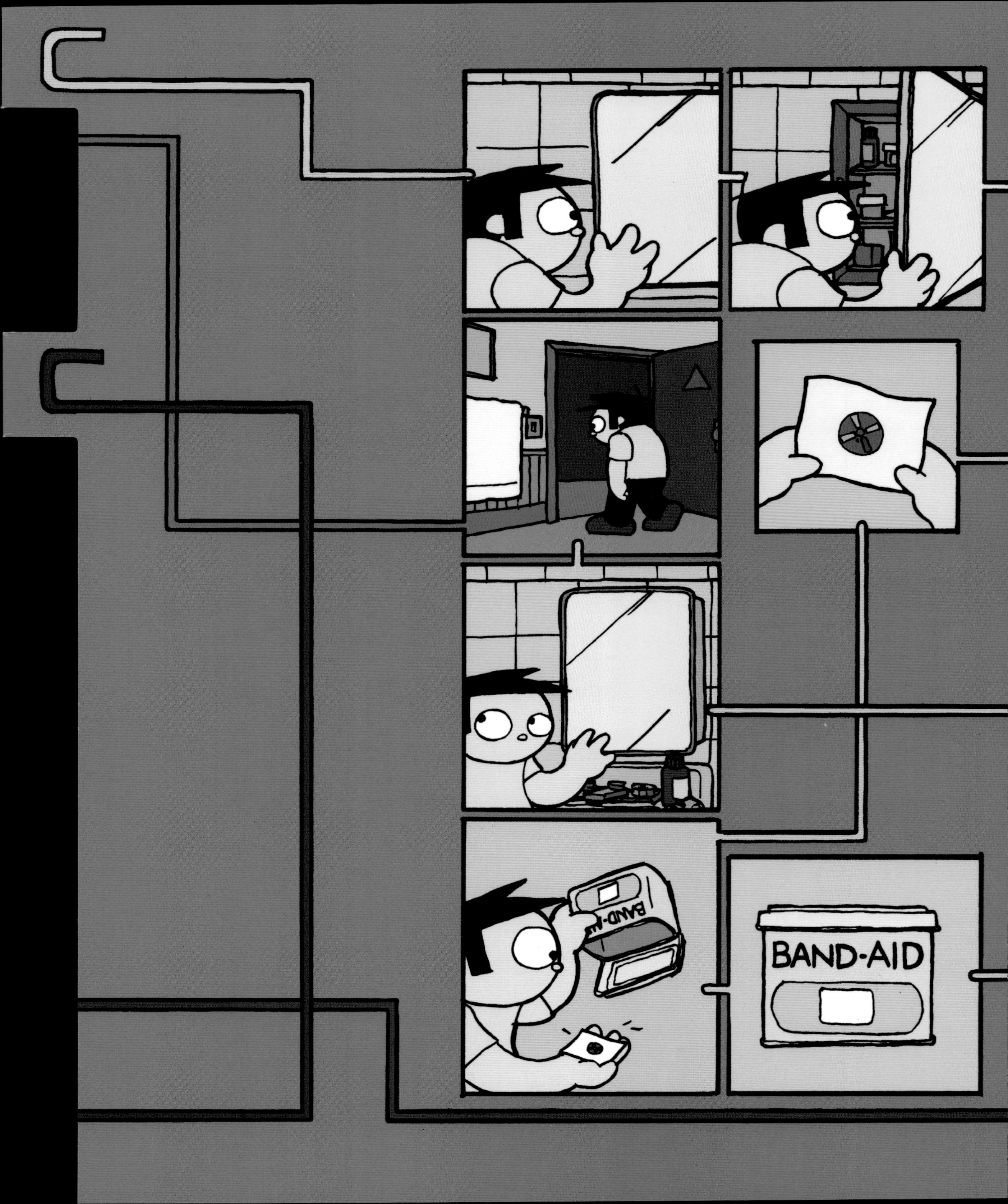
BAND-AID

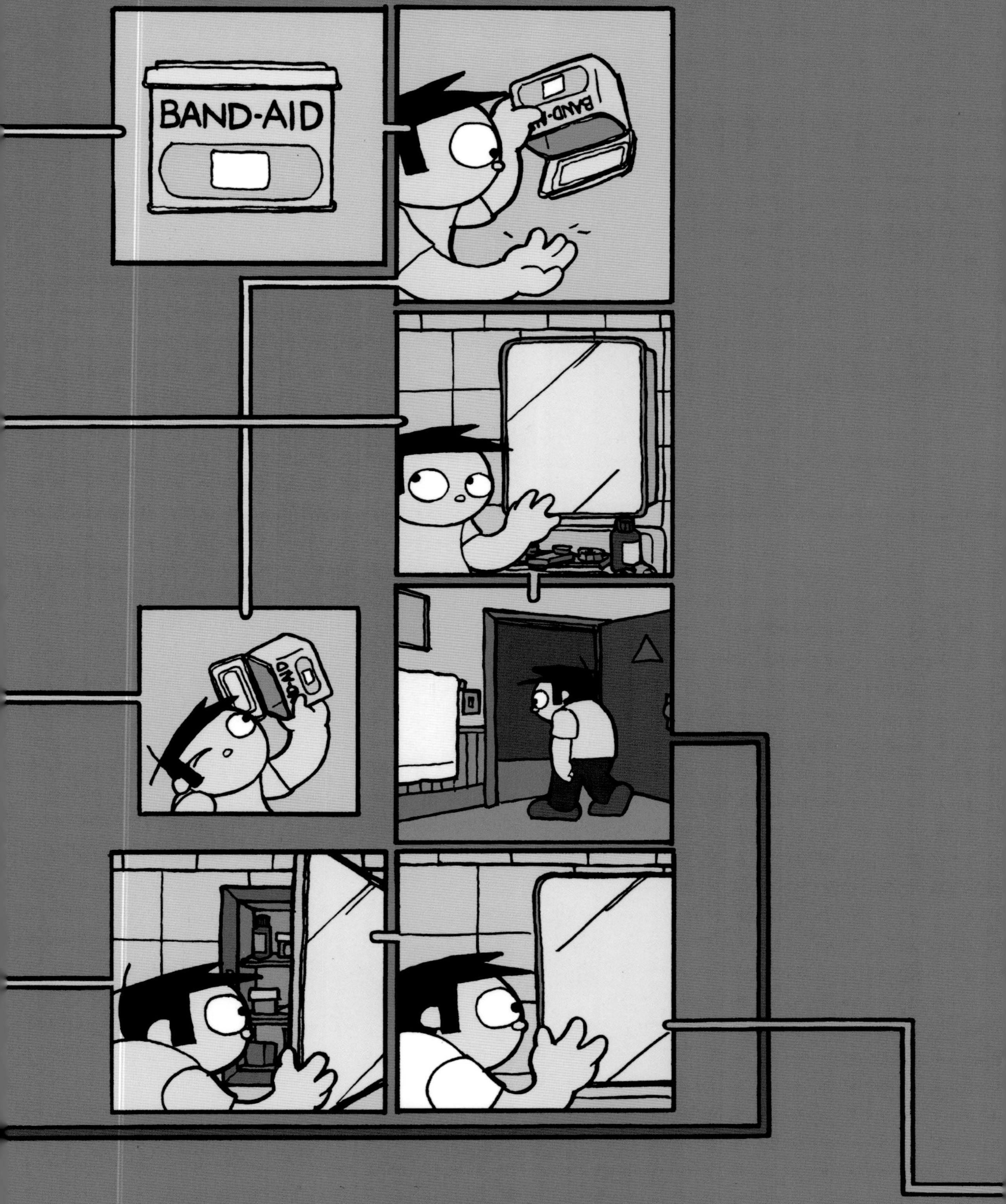
BAND-AID

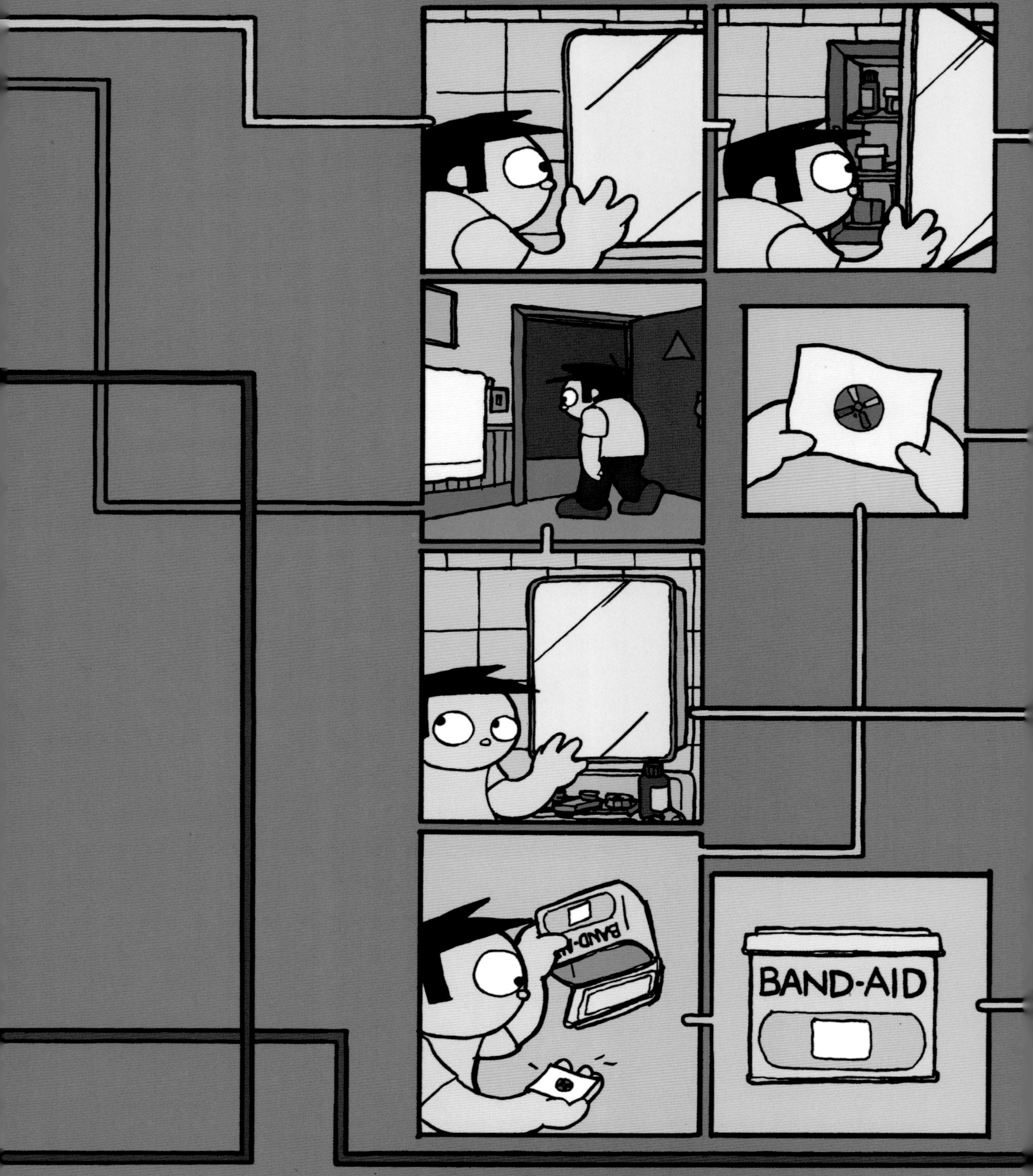
BAND-AID

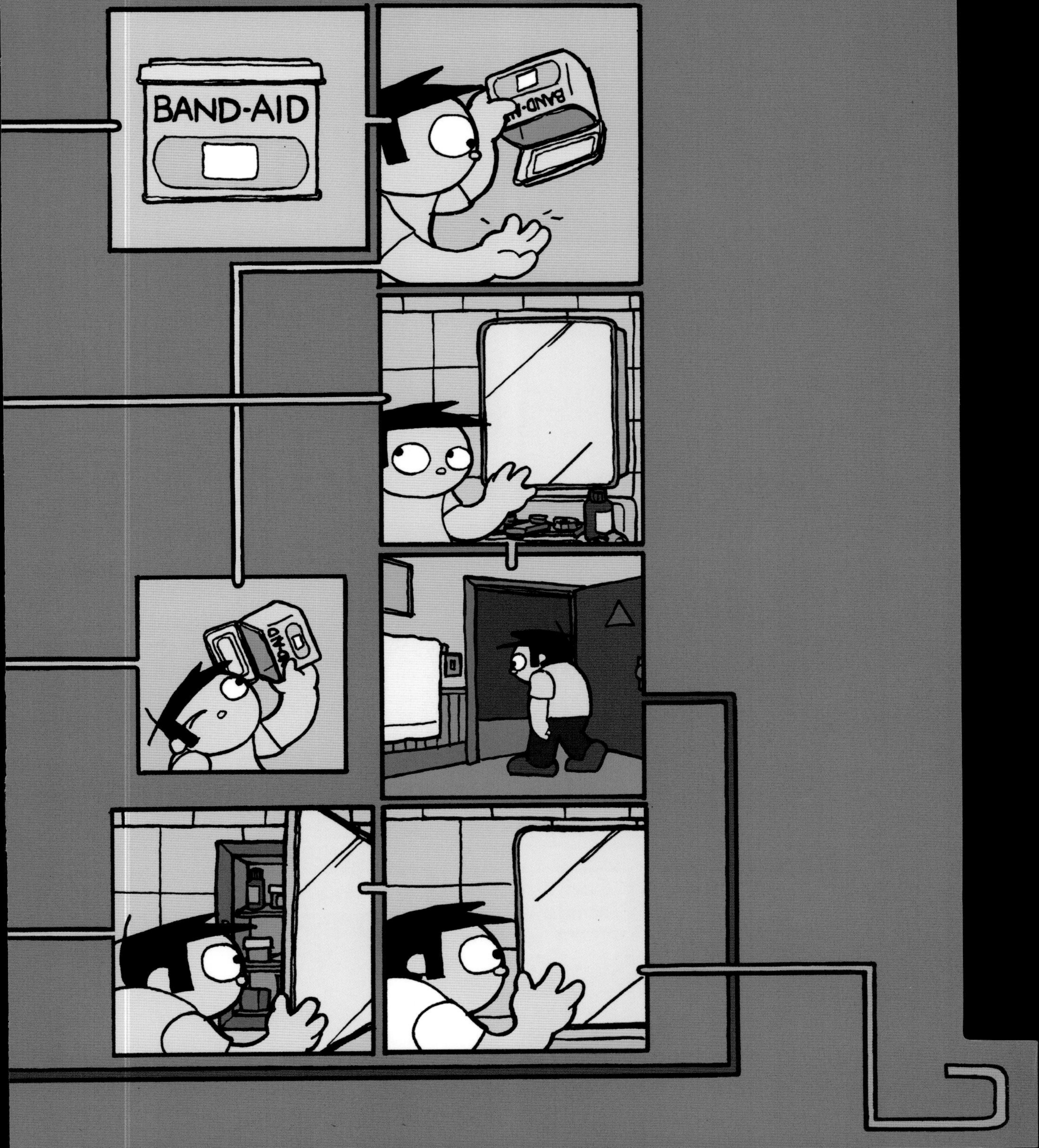
BAND-AID

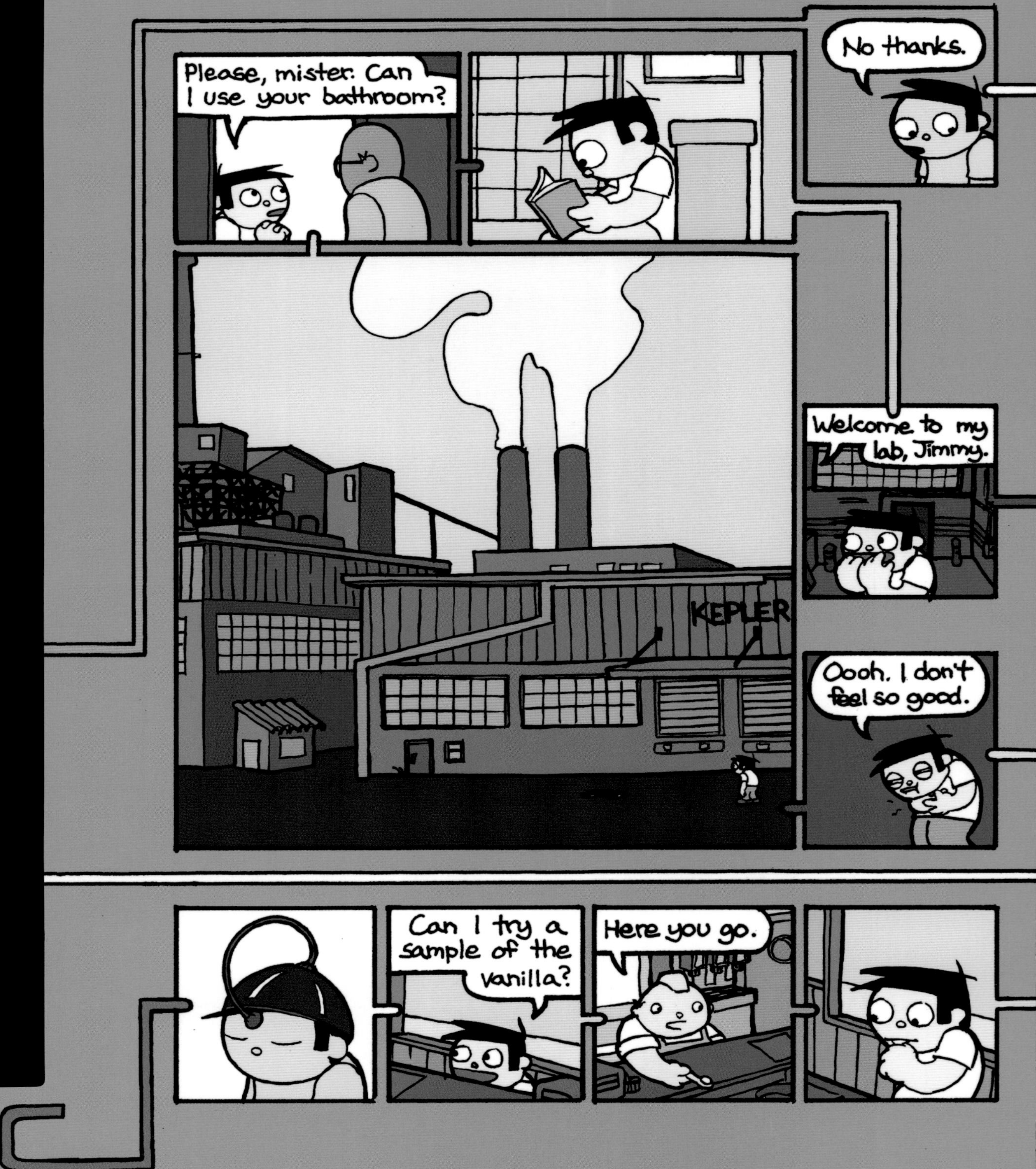
Please, mister. Can I use your bathroom?
No thanks.
KEPLER
Welcome to my lab, Jimmy.
Oooh. I don't feel so good.
Can I try a sample of the vanilla?
Here you go.

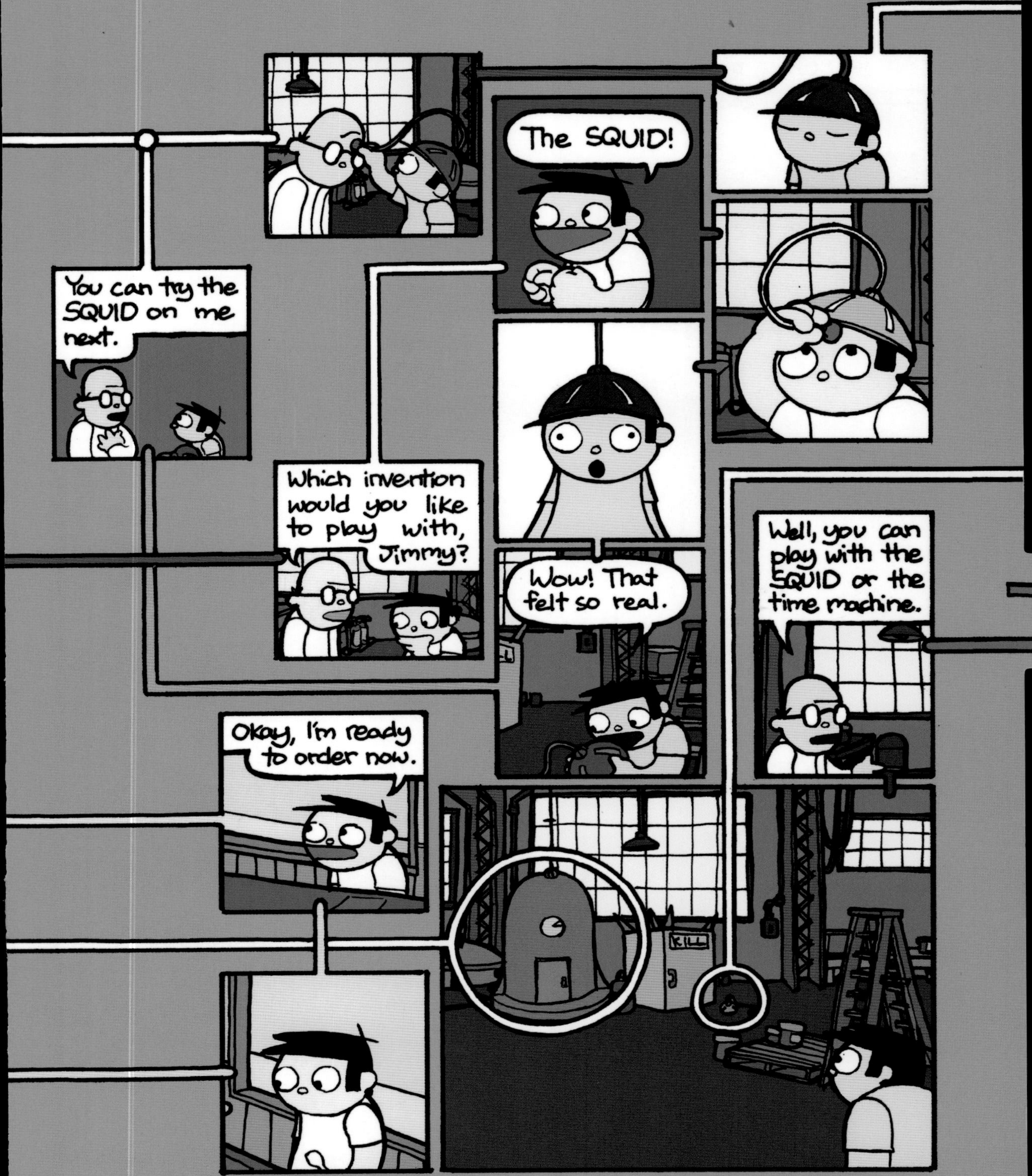
The SQUID!
You can try the SQUID on me next.
Which invention would you like to play with, Jimmy?
Well, you can play with the SQUID or the time machine.
Wow! That felt so real.
Okay, I'm ready to order now.
KILL

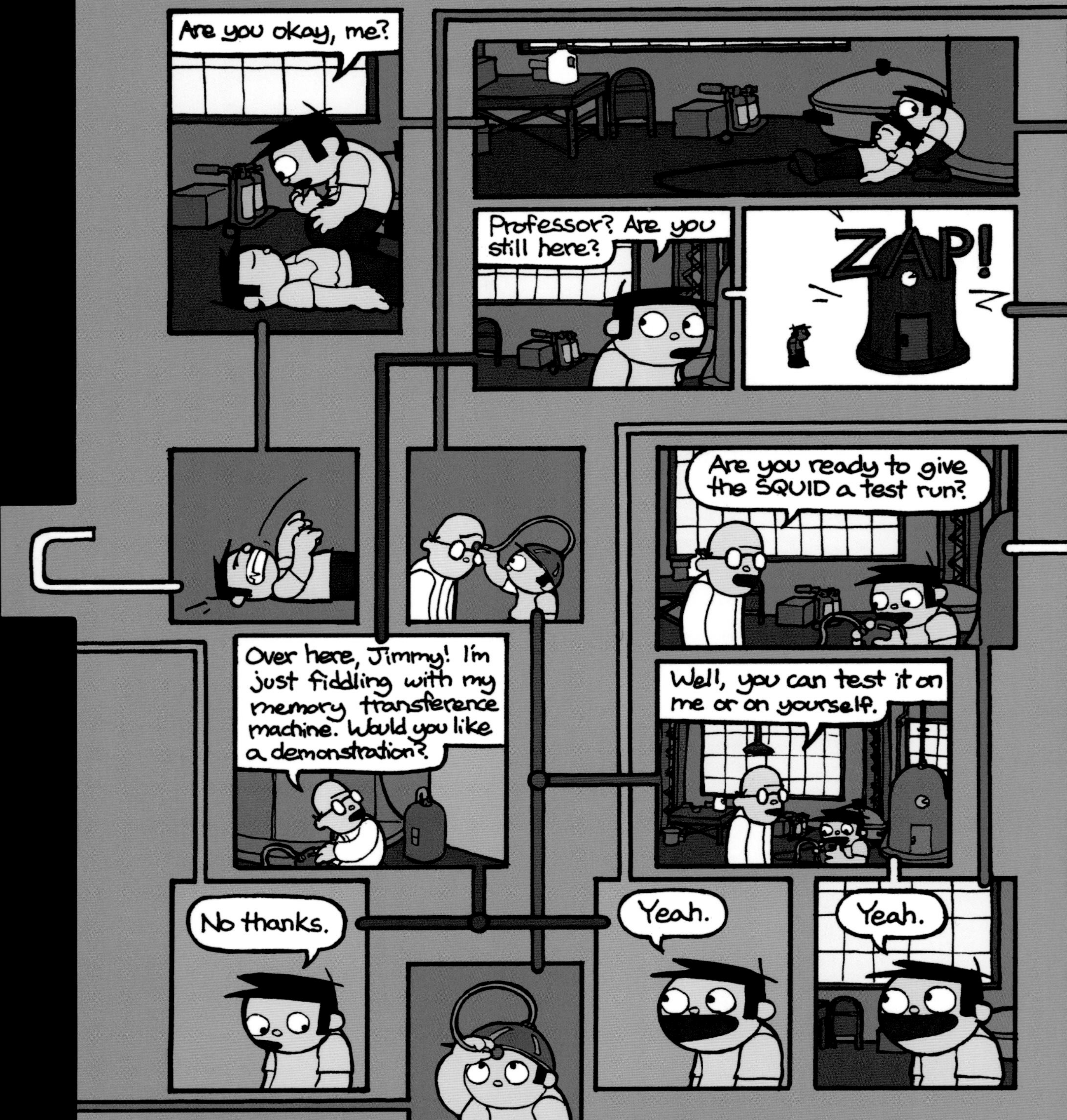
Are you okay, me?
Professor? Are you still here?
ZAP!
Are you ready to give the SQUID a test run?
Over here, Jimmy! I'm just fiddling with my memory transference machine. Would you like a demonstration?
Well, you can test it on me or on yourself.
No thanks.
Yeah.
Yeah.

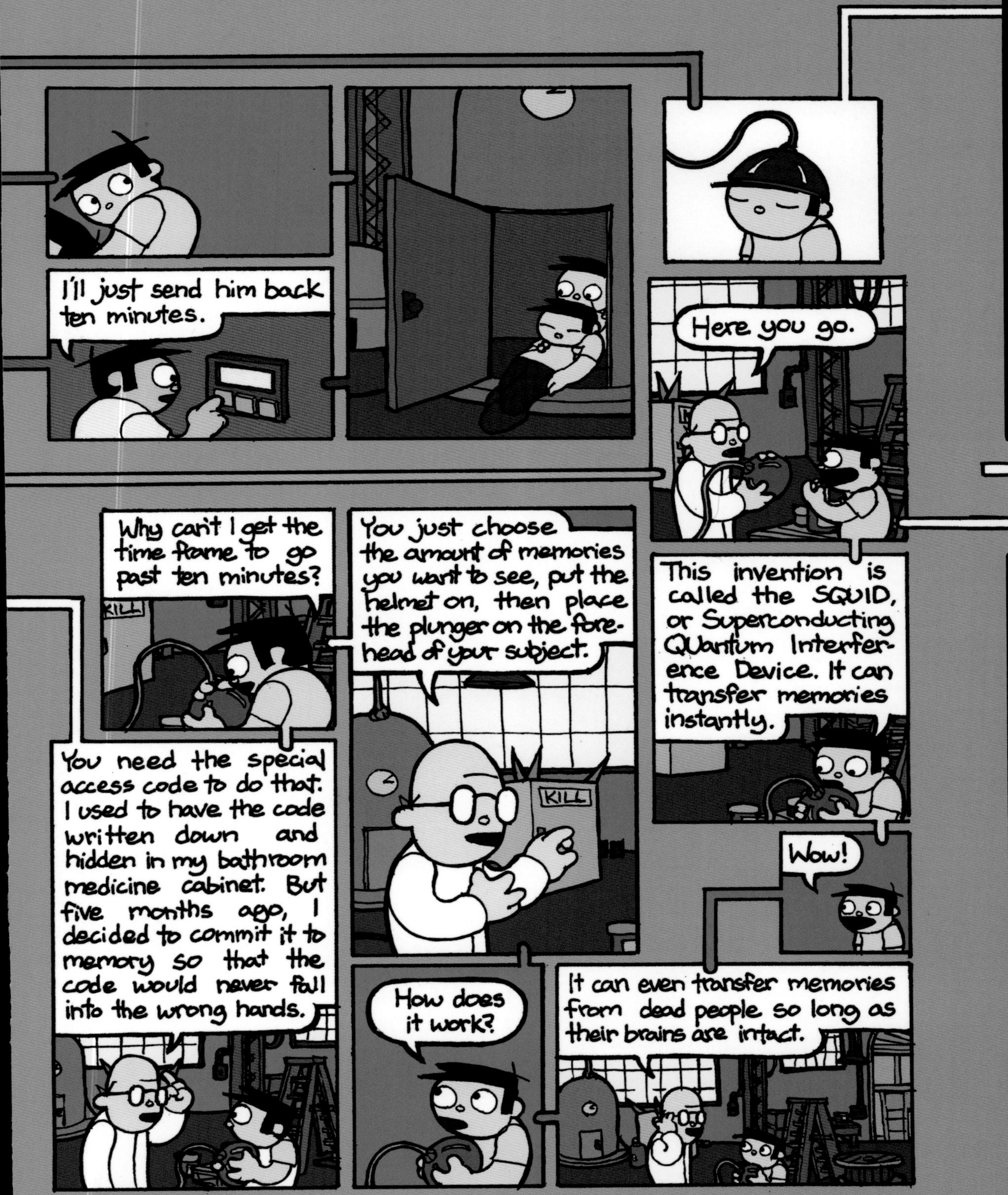
I'll just send him back ten minutes.
Here you go.
This invention is called the SQUID, or Superconducting QUantum Interference Device. It can transfer memories instantly.
Wow!
It can even transfer memories from dead people so long as their brains are intact.
How does it work?
You just choose the amount of memories you want to see, put the helmet on, then place the plunger on the forehead of your subject.
KILL
Why can't I get the time frame to go past ten minutes?
KILL
You need the special access code to do that. I used to have the code written down and hidden in my bathroom medicine cabinet. But five months ago, I decided to commit it to memory so that the code would never fall into the wrong hands.

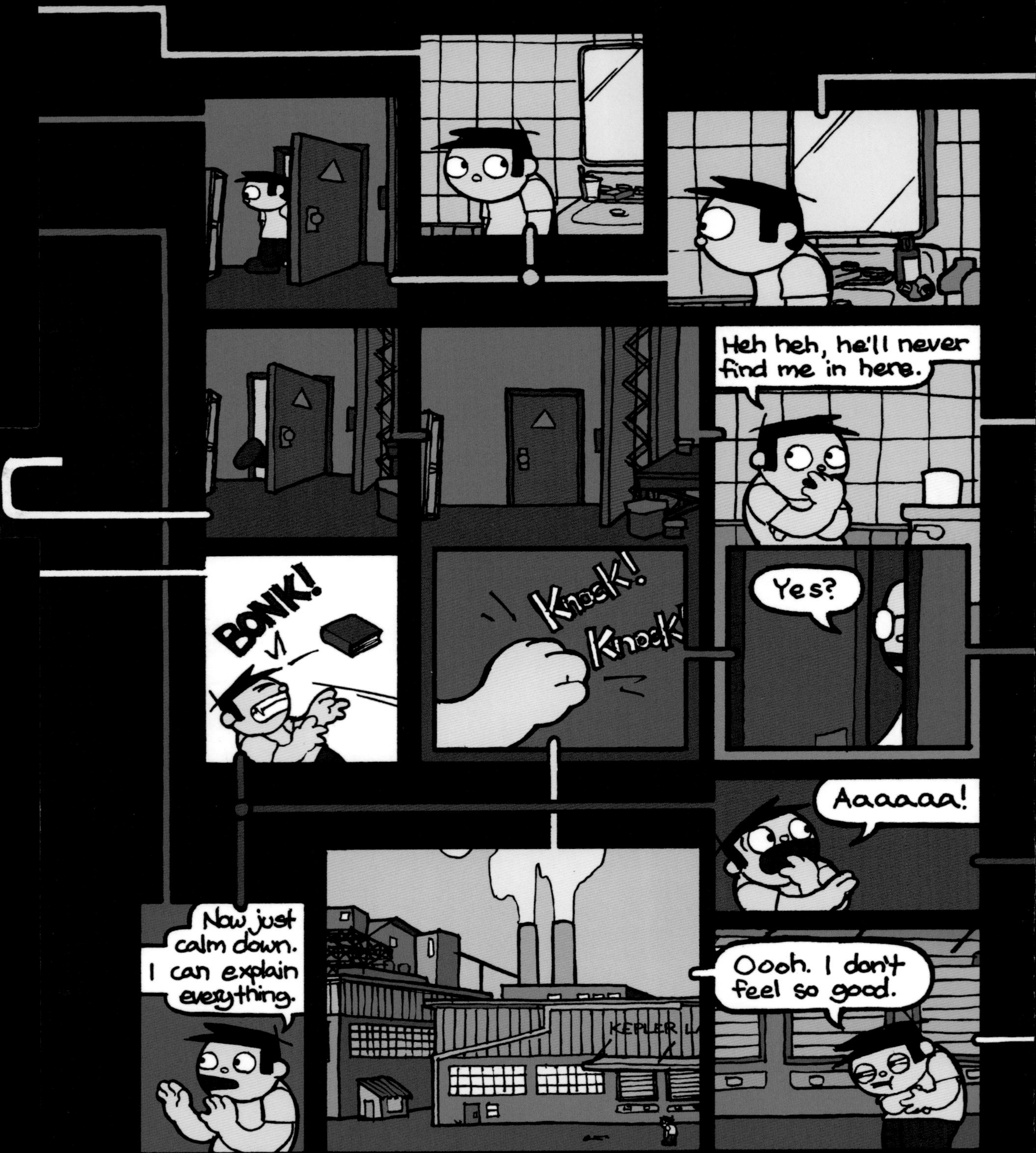

Heh heh, he'll never find me in here.
BONK!
Knock!
Knock!
Yes?
Aaaaaa!
Now just calm down. I can explain everything.
KEPLER LA
Oooh. I don't feel so good.

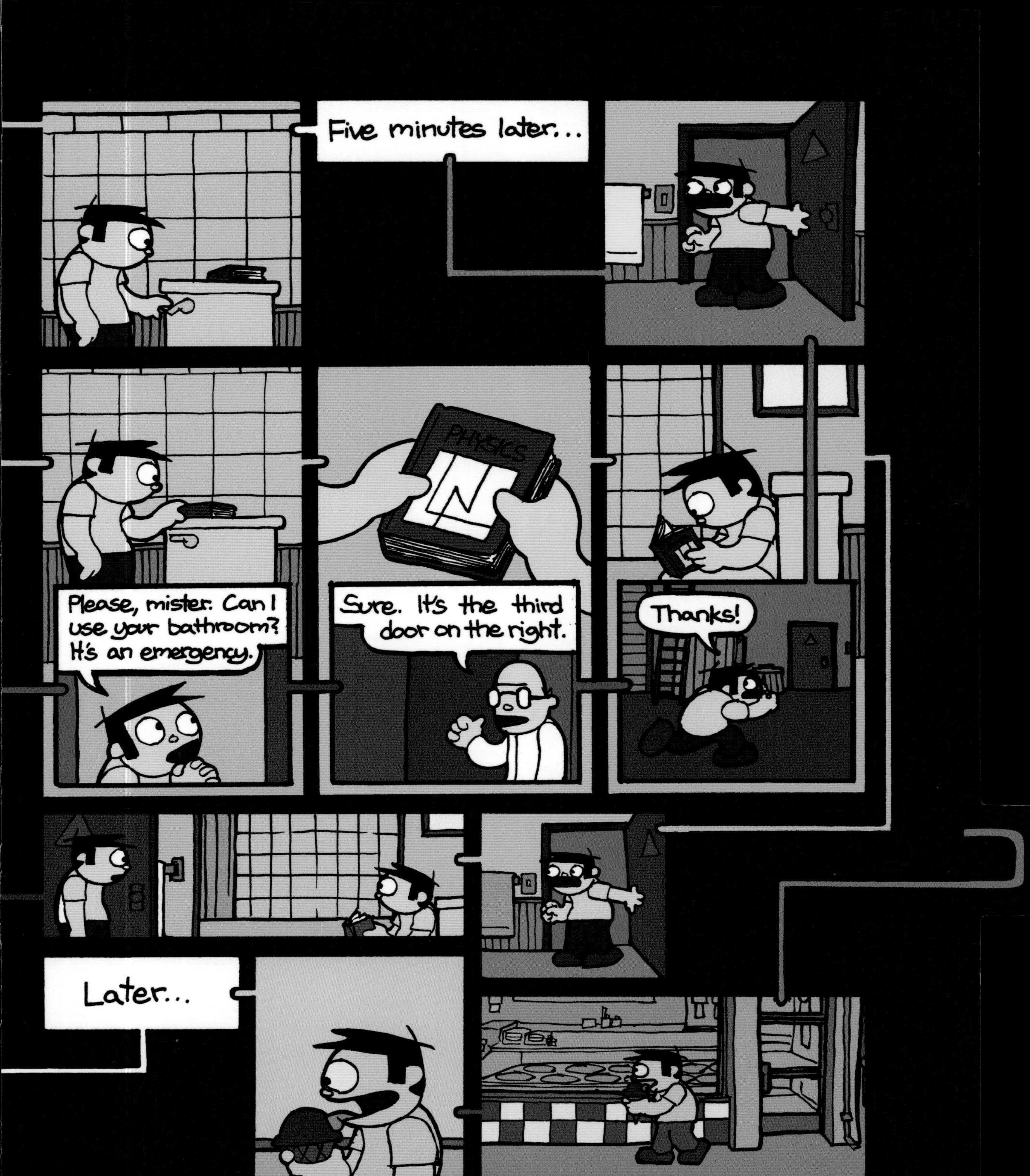
Five minutes later...
PHYSICS
Please, mister: Can I use your bathroom? It's an emergency.
Sure. It's the third door on the right.
Thanks!
Later...

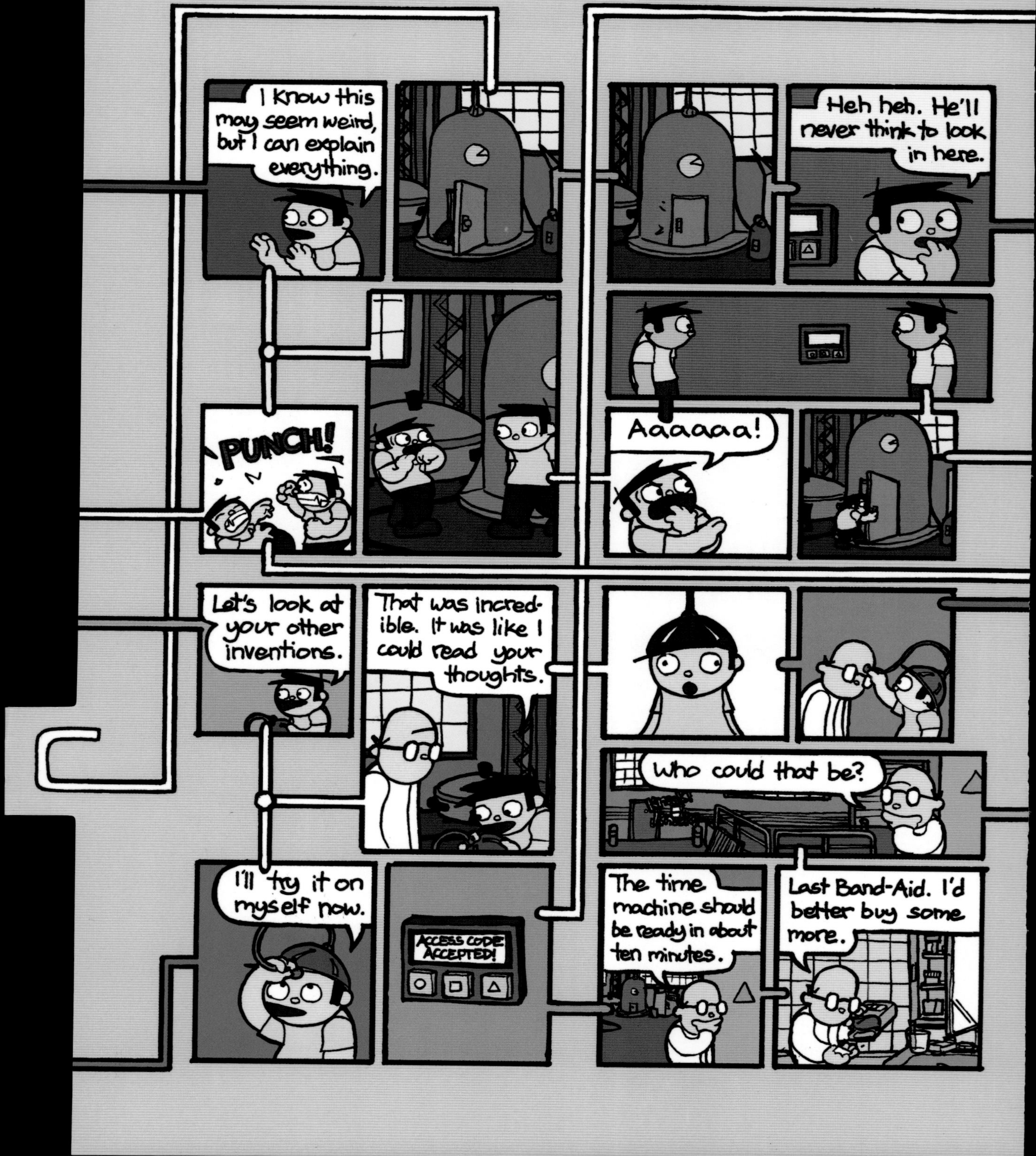
I know this may seem weird, but I can explain everything.
Heh heh. He'll never think to look in here.
PUNCH!
Aaaaaa!
Let's look at your other inventions.
That was incred-ible. It was like I could read your thoughts.
Who could that be?
I'll try it on myself now.
ACCESS CODE ACCEPTED!
The time machine should be ready in about ten minutes.
Last Band-Aid. I'd better buy some more.

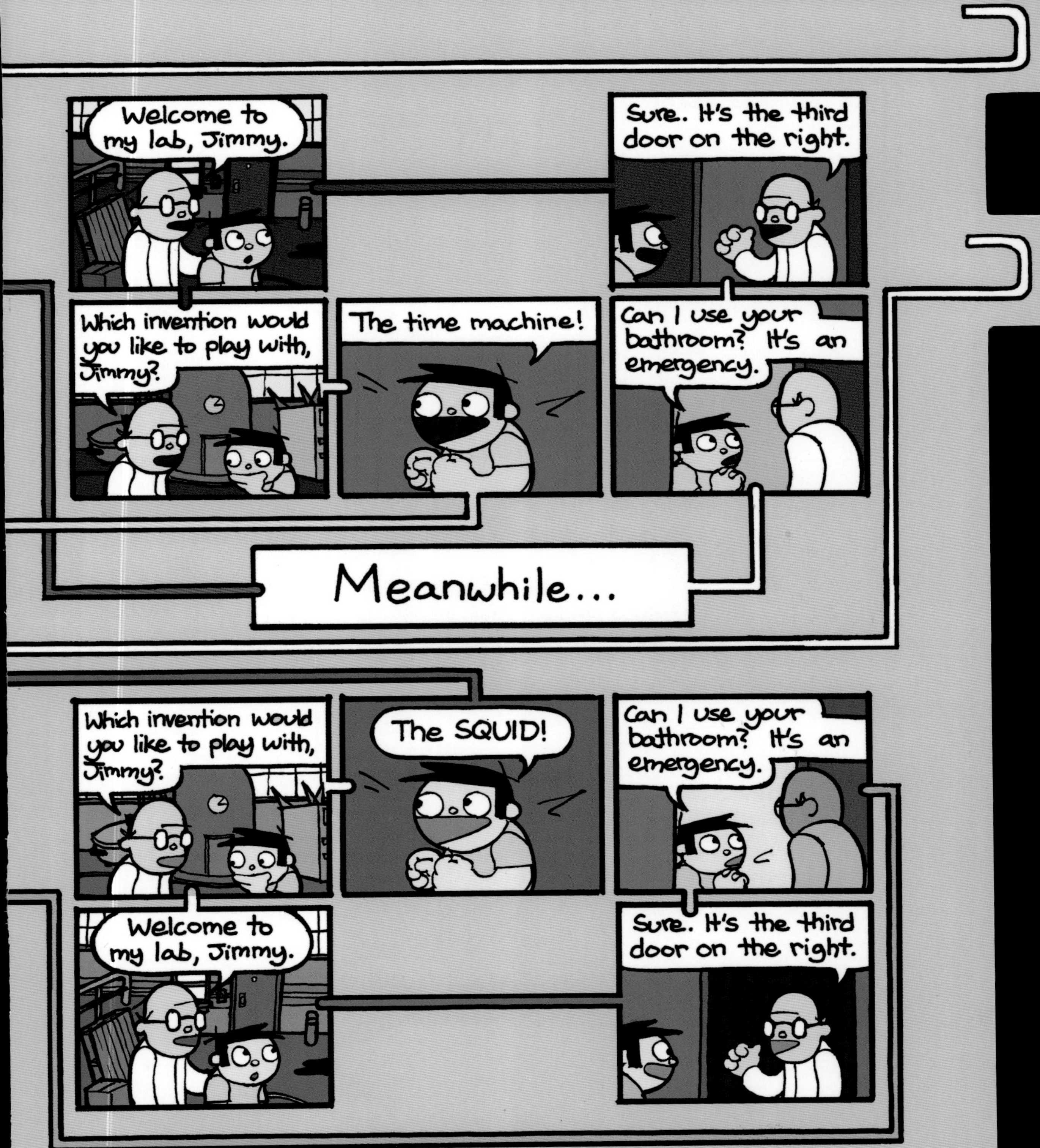
Welcome to my lab, Jimmy.
Sure. It's the third door on the right.
Which invention would you like to play with, Jimmy?
The time machine!
Can I use your bathroom? It's an emergency.
Meanwhile...
Which invention would you like to play with, Jimmy?
The SQUID!
Can I use your bathroom? It's an emergency.
Welcome to my lab, Jimmy.
Sure. It's the third door on the right.

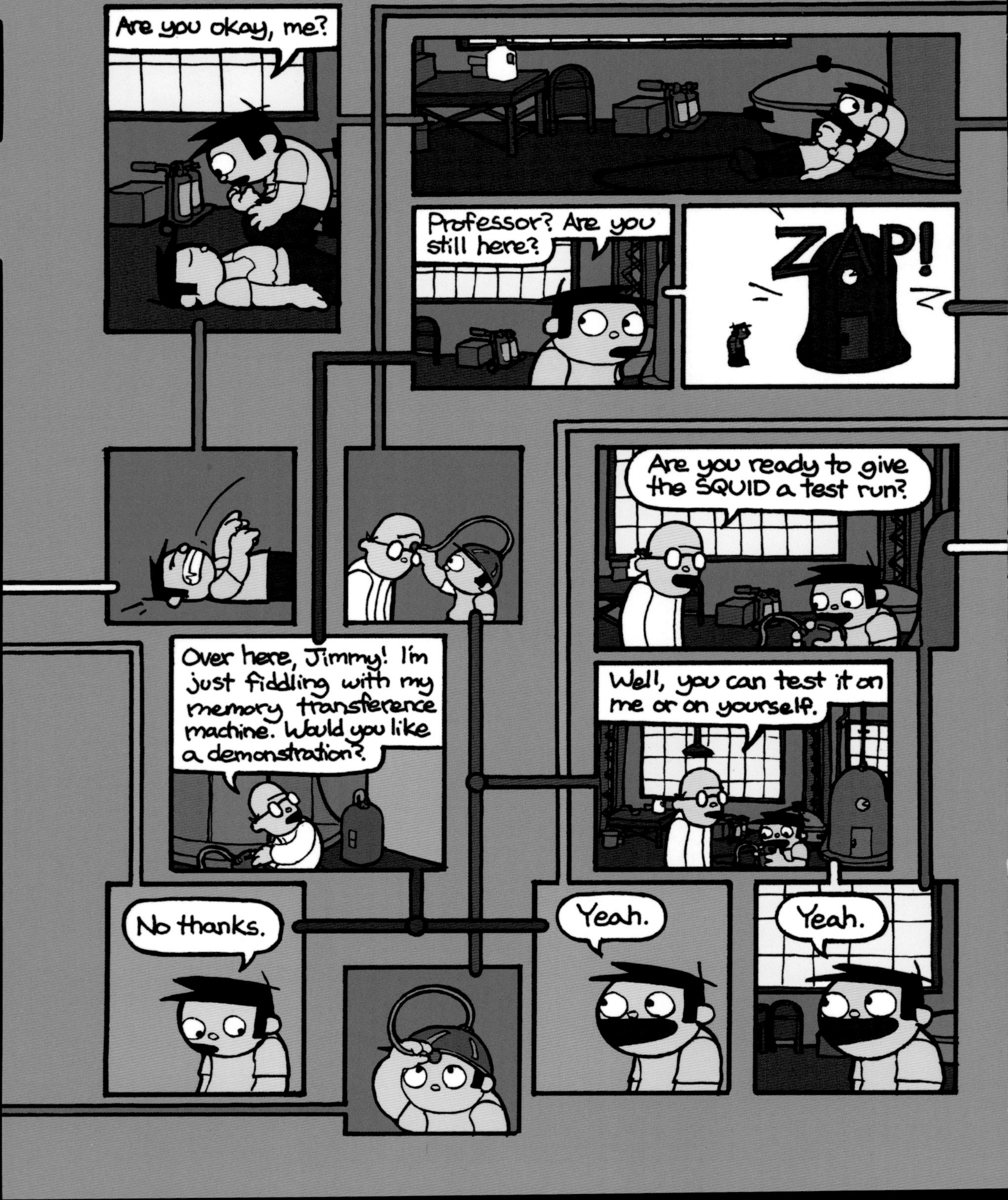
Are you okay, me?
Professor? Are you still here?
ZAP!
Are you ready to give the SQUID a test run?
Over here, Jimmy! I'm just fiddling with my memory transference machine. Would you like a demonstration?
Well, you can test it on me or on yourself.
No thanks.
Yeah.
Yeah.

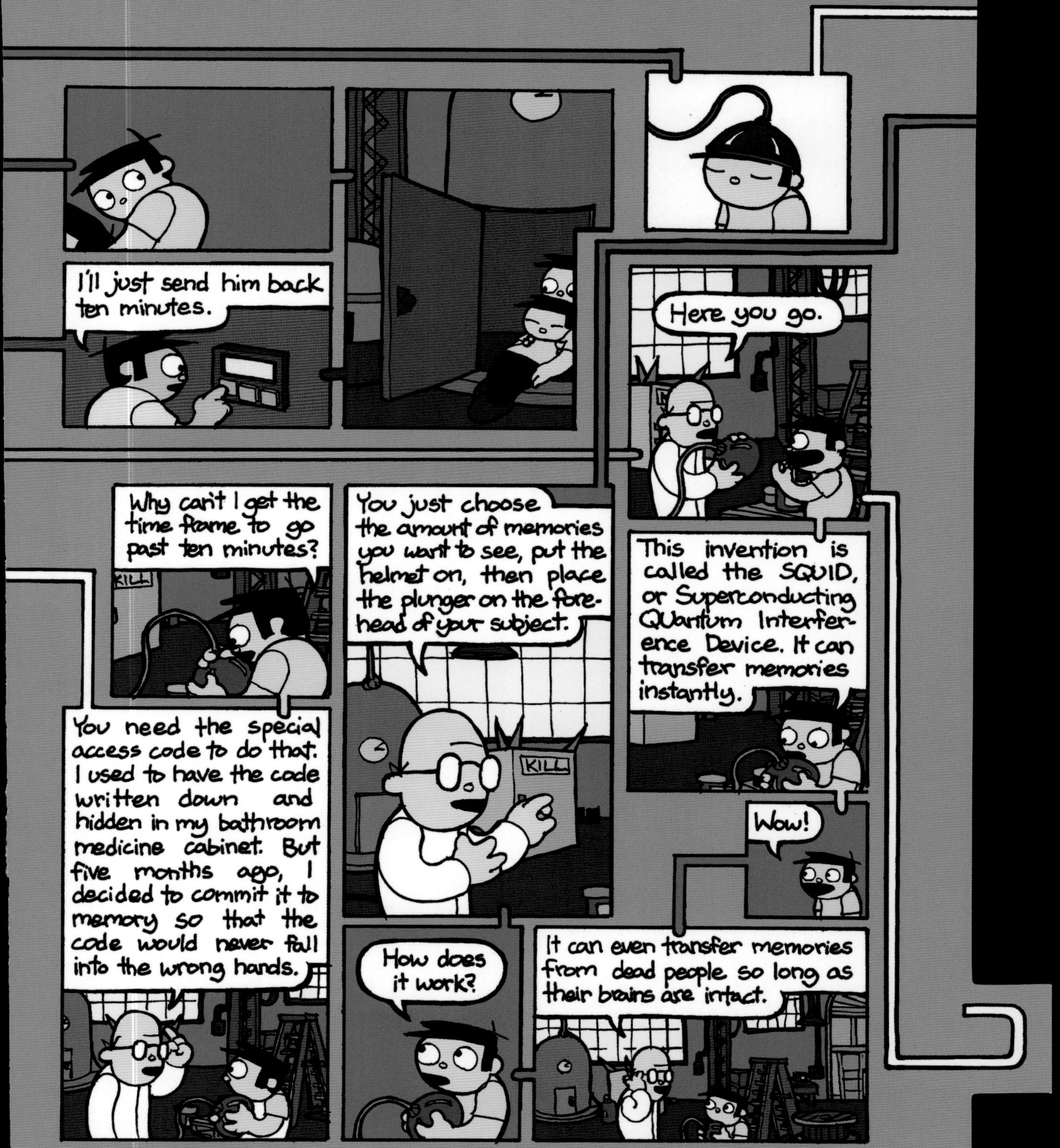
I'll just send him back ten minutes.
Here you go.
This invention is called the SQUID, or Superconducting QUantum Interference Device. It can transfer memories instantly.
Wow!
It can even transfer memories from dead people so long as their brains are intact.
How does it work?
You just choose the amount of memories you want to see, put the helmet on, then place the plunger on the forehead of your subject.
KILL
Why can't I get the time frame to go past ten minutes?
KILL
You need the special access code to do that. I used to have the code written down and hidden in my bathroom medicine cabinet. But five months ago, I decided to commit it to memory so that the code would never fall into the wrong hands.

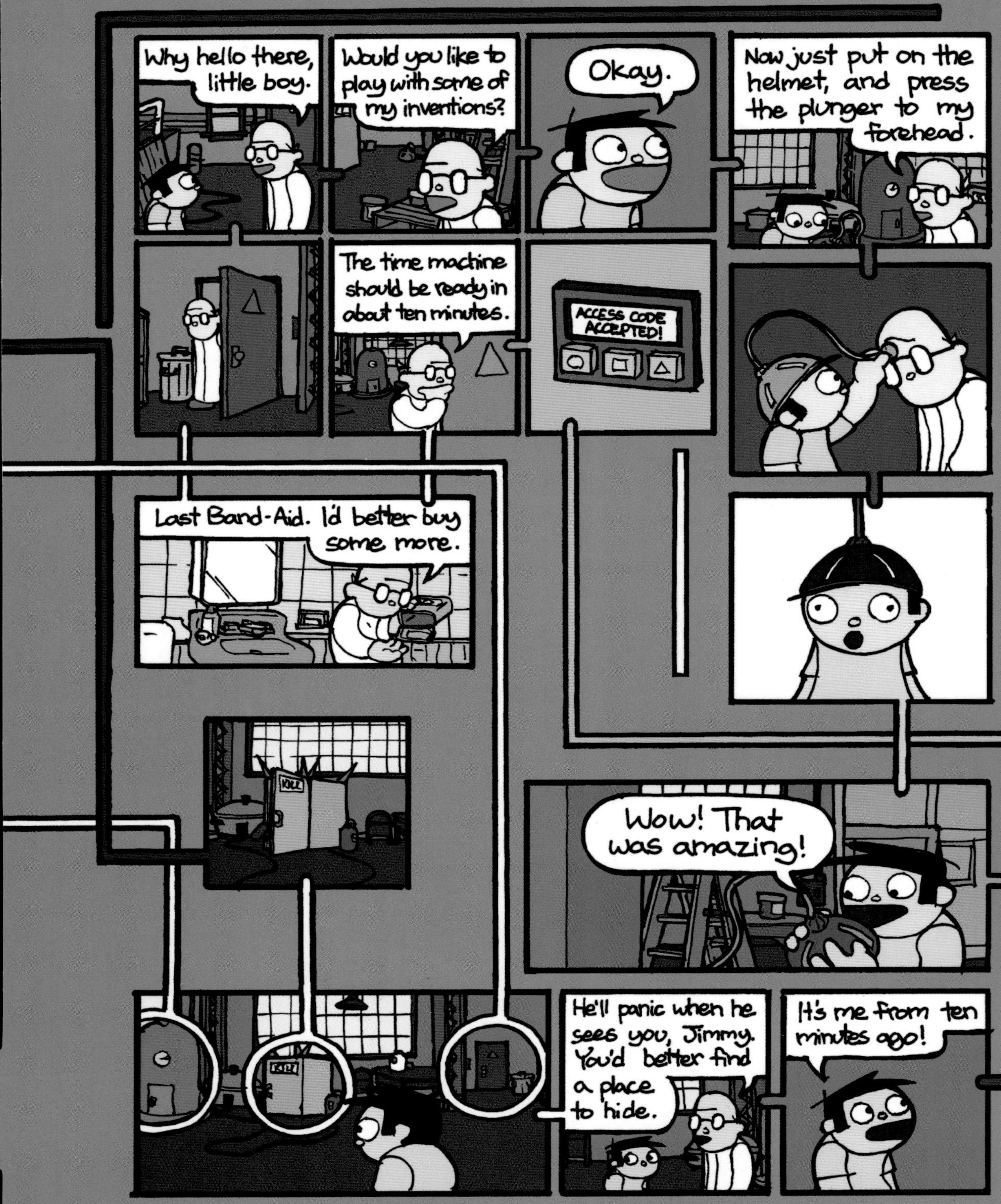
Why hello there, little boy.
Would you like to play with some of my inventions?
Okay.
Now just put on the helmet, and press the plunger to my forehead.
The time machine should be ready in about ten minutes.
ACCESS CODE ACCEPTED!
Last Band-Aid. I'd better buy some more.
Wow! That was amazing!
He'll panic when he sees you, Jimmy. You'd better find a place to hide.
It's me from ten minutes ago!

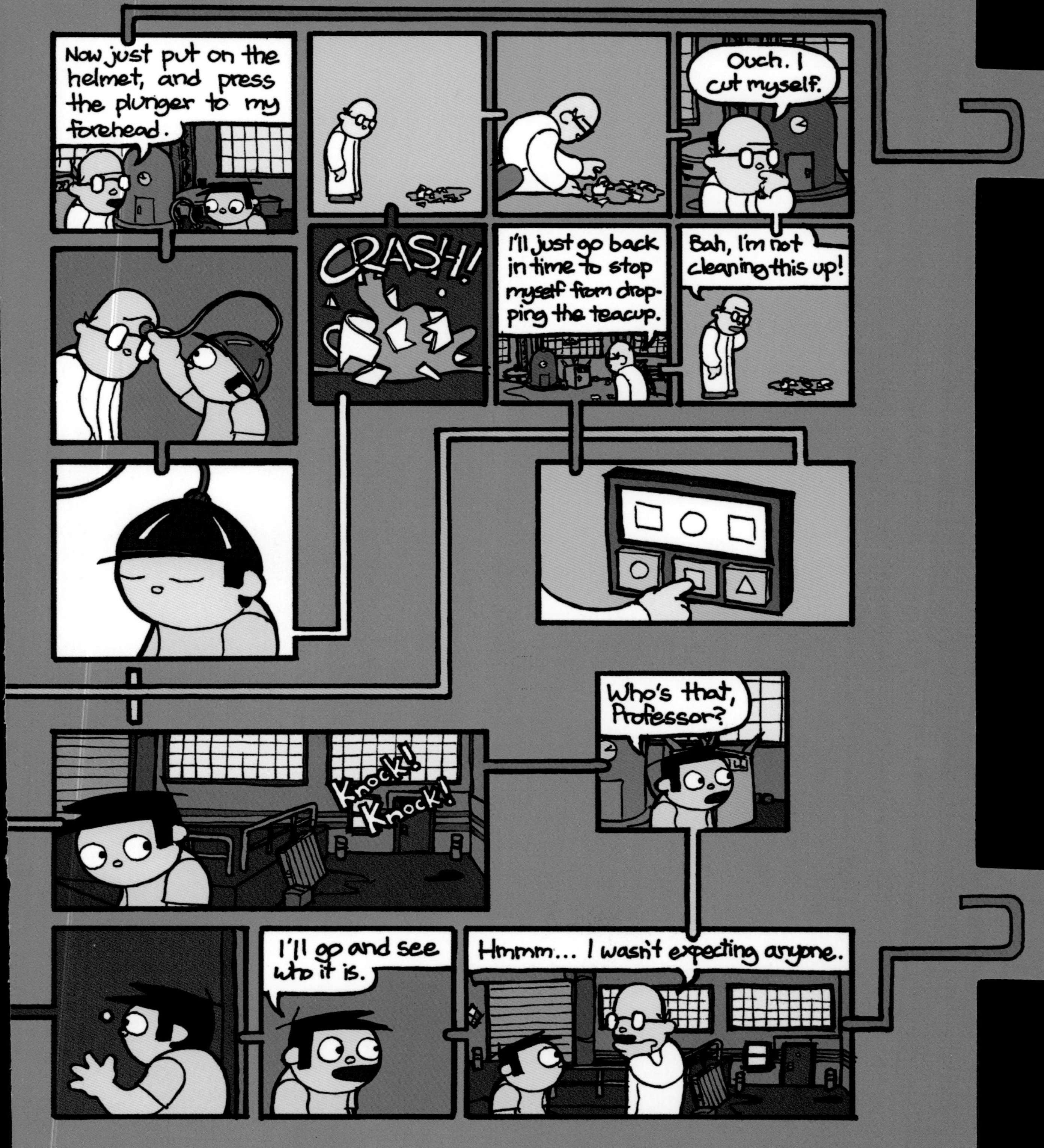
Now just put on the helmet, and press the plunger to my forehead.
Ouch. I cut myself.
CRASH!
I'll just go back in time to stop myself from dropping the teacup.
Bah, I'm not cleaning this up!
Knock! Knock!
Who's that, Professor?
I'll go and see who it is.
Hmmm... I wasn't expecting anyone.

JASON SHIGA

graduated from the University of California at Berkeley with a degree in pure mathematics. He is the author of more than twenty comic books and the inventor of three board games, two card tricks, the greedy mug, the bus clock, and the world's second-largest interactive comic, which spanned twenty-five square feet. His puzzles and mazes have appeared in *McSweeny's* and *Nick Magazine*. He lives in Oakland, California.